End of Story

A Village Library Mystery, Volume 9

Elizabeth Spann Craig

Published by Elizabeth Spann Craig, 2023.

This is a work of fiction. Similarities to real people, places, or events are entirely coincidental.

END OF STORY

First edition. June 27, 2023.

Written by Elizabeth Spann Craig.

Thanks, Johnny!

Chapter One

I decided it was way too early in the morning to have a conversation with Zelda. Zelda, my homeowner association president and library volunteer, was actually not really engaged in conversation at all. It was more of con*sternations*. A litany of complaints. Since we were present at the library, the complaints centered on patrons, one in particular.

Zelda growled, "He's talking too loud. He's practically yelling."

I explained, "We only worry about volume in the quiet area, remember? People can talk at ordinary levels everywhere else."

Zelda sniffed. "Nothing ordinary about his level. Anyway, I didn't say he was talking. He's listening to stuff on his phone."

I frowned. "Okay. Well, patrons do need to wear headphones if they're listening to media. That's just a matter of being respectful to other people around them. Is there anyone near him?"

"*I* was near him," said Zelda with disdain. "Can't shelve books when he's being that loud."

I bit back a sigh. "Would you like me to ask him to use headphones?"

"Nope. I'll do it." Zelda squared her shoulders and headed toward the unfortunate patron.

"Politely!" I pleaded as she stomped in his direction.

Another loud voice assailed Zelda's ears, and she whirled around to glare at Luna, my friend and the children's librarian. Luna clapped a hand over her mouth and winked at Zelda, who shot her a cold look and proceeded to stomp over to the loud patron.

Luna not only sounded loud, she looked loud, too. Always in wildly colorful clothes, she sported a tie-dye tunic with bright blue pants and multicolored tennis shoes. Her hair was currently yellow. Not blonde, but the type of yellow you might see road crews wearing on safety vests. Somehow, the contrasting hues looked perfect on her. She was the only person I knew who could pull them all off.

"Hey, your seed library is a huge success," said Luna, beaming at me.

We'd started a seed library where patrons could bring seedlings or seeds and take home others to grow at home during swaps that we held. We'd made modified greenhouses, putting one in the children's department, and one in the adult area.

"Is it?" I was pleased to hear this.

"The kids love looking at all the plants growing. They've been checking out more science-related books, too, to learn more about them. It's pretty cool."

Wilson, our uptight library director, overheard Luna and stopped. He looked pleased, which was always a good thing. When Wilson wasn't pleased with library engagement, it could make life difficult. He'd think up programs, ask for more social media posts, and generally make himself an agitated mess.

"You're saying the plants are working well in the children's department?" he asked.

Luna grinned at him. "You need to hang out over there with me. Kids of all ages are checking it out. The little guys peer inside the greenhouses with their moms. The teens are even keeping up with how much the plants are growing and what they're turning into."

Wilson raised his eyebrows. "Even the teens," he murmured.

Luna and I smiled at each other. The teen patrons always seemed to be a mystery to Wilson. Consequently, he was especially eager to get them engaged at the library. He asked a few more questions about what types of science books were being checked out and what kids were saying about the greenhouse. Then he said, "That's all good."

I felt myself relax at this pronouncement. But then Wilson added, "I only wish I felt as confident over Ann's upcoming vacation."

Luna rolled her eyes at me. To Wilson, she said, "The library is going to be just fine. We've divided up Ann's duties. She has an autoresponder set up for her email address. And she's coming *back*, Wilson. She's only gone for two weeks. I'm not sure Ann has ever really taken a vacation before."

Wilson opened his mouth to refute this, then paused, frowning. "Have you, Ann?"

I shrugged. "I've taken some long weekends from time-to-time."

Luna said in a scolding tone, "That's not much of a break. By the time the long weekend is over, you've just started to relax. Then you have to go right back to work."

"I like it here," I said, shrugging again.

Wilson beamed at me. Those were the words he most enjoyed hearing.

Zelda, who'd returned from telling off the patron, glared at us. I wasn't sure if the glare was because we were talking or because there was mention of my vacation. Zelda was a tremendous proponent of work. She and Wilson actually had a lot in common, despite some obvious differences.

Zelda took an unexpected detour into our conversation. She growled, "You're going out of town?"

"Grayson and I are going to Charleston together," I said. Grayson was my boyfriend and a neighbor of both Zelda and mine.

"Ann, you gotta fill out a proxy vote before you go. And Grayson does, too."

I hastily nodded. "Right, right. I'll remind Grayson. And I promise I'll slip that in your mailbox." Zelda was referring to the proxy vote for the homeowner association's officer elections.

Zelda scowled at me. "Not *in* the mailbox. That's against federal law."

Luna's eyes twinkled. "You're committing felonies now, Ann? You're out of control."

Zelda continued severely, "Put it in the newspaper slot underneath the mailbox." Giving us all a final look of disapproval, she sniffed and pushed her cart off to do more shelving.

Fitz, the library cat, had been watching Zelda with interest on his furry face. I could understand why; she was particularly animated today. He walked over and rubbed against my legs to get some reassurance. I reached down to pet him.

Wilson said slowly, "Who's going to take care of Fitz while you're gone? Are you going to leave him here in the library?"

Fitz had originally stayed at the library overnight. But soon after, I realized how much I enjoyed having the furry guy at home with me. Now I carted Fitz back and forth from my house to the library and home again on the days I worked.

"I'm taking him with me to Charleston," I said.

Wilson frowned. "He'll be good in the car for that long?"

Fitz gave Wilson a disappointed look.

I said, "Fitz is always *perfect* in the car. He got used to it when he was a kitten, so now he doesn't think twice."

Wilson said, "Your hotel won't mind having a cat stay? I've heard of dog-friendly hotels, but I've never heard of cat-friendly ones."

"Oh, Grayson and I are staying with a friend of mine there. She insisted I bring Fitz along. She's a big cat-lover."

Wilson said rather gloomily, "At least it sounds like everything will work out on your end. I only hope things will work out as well on ours."

"Everything is going to be *great*," said Luna. "We're fully staffed. Plus, poor Ann has been working overtime to get the library newsletter scheduled in advance and all the library's social media. It'll be like she's still here!"

I gave Luna a wryly grateful look. Wilson was always a worrywart with staffing issues. Plus, he acted like I was the only one who knew how to do anything at the library. If it hadn't been so annoying, it would have been a compliment.

Wilson said, "All right. Hopefully, it will all go as well as you're thinking it will, Luna." With that, he strode grimly back to his office.

Luna snorted. "He's such a fun-loving guy. Ann, I swear, if he makes you worry about *anything* during your well-deserved break, I'm going to wring his neck."

I grinned at her. "Oh, the library is going to be out-of-sight, out-of-mind as soon as I get to Charleston. I mean, I love all of you. But I could definitely use some vacation time." I frowned and quickly amended, "Of course, it's not all going to be fun and games."

Luna said, "Remind me again why Grayson needs to make this trip. It was something to do with a death in the family, right?"

"Right. It was an uncle of his. He honestly barely remembers him from when he was a kid. But Grayson got a call a couple of weeks ago from an attorney. He told him his uncle had made him the beneficiary of his estate."

Luna quirked an eyebrow. "Sounds like an unexpected surprise."

"He was totally flabbergasted. He thought there might be some sort of mistake. He also wondered why his dad wasn't getting the inheritance instead of him."

"Sounds like a mystery," said Luna. "Was there a falling-out between his dad and his uncle?"

"Apparently not. The lawyer didn't want to disclose too much until he met with him in person, but he did say that the fact Grayson is a newspaper editor really appealed to him. The lawyer said his uncle had been a journalist for a while."

Zelda, passing by with her book cart, shot Luna and me a dirty look.

"We'd better get back to work or else Zelda will have our heads," I murmured as we scurried away.

The rest of the day went by like a blur. That spoke less to the fact that I was thinking about my upcoming vacation and more to the fact that everything in the library that could break, broke. The copier and the printer both went on the fritz as if they'd made a pact. A toilet in the restroom overflowed. Then the internet went down, which qualified as a bona fide emergency in every way. When the day was finally over, I left the library, Fitz in tow, with a sense of relief.

Back at the house, Fitz and I looked at my suitcase sprawled on my bed. Fitz decided he could best help me by climbing into the suitcase and lying on top of the packing cubes. I rubbed him under his chin and he closed his eyes most of the way in enjoyment.

"That's so helpful, Fitz," I said fondly. "Luckily, I can check my packing list and make sure I put everything in there," I said to him affectionately. Fitz curled up with his tail over his face and promptly fell asleep.

I glanced over at my list. It looked like everything was either in my suitcase or in one of my tote bags. I had a couple of semi-dressy outfits, shorts and tee shirts, and several bathing suits. We were going to be doing a variety of different things, but my friend Holly also had a washer and dryer at her place, so I didn't have to pack a ton of stuff.

My phone rang. Fitz opened a single eye, looked reprovingly at my cell phone, and closed it firmly again.

"Grayson," I said, smiling as I picked up.

"I'm guessing you're a hundred percent packed and checking your packing list," said Grayson in a teasing tone.

I laughed. "Do you have hidden cameras trained on me or something?"

"No, I've just gotten to know you pretty well."

I felt a fissure of happiness course through me. It felt *good* to be well known. It also wasn't something I was totally accustomed to. I said, "Let me guess where you are with your packing."

"I have the funny feeling you might have a pretty good idea."

I said, "Hmm. I'm guessing you've pulled the suitcase out of the closet and have it open to give you inspiration."

There was now a full-fledged laugh on the other end of the line. He said in a rueful tone, "You know me too well. I was planning on getting started with packing yesterday, but just didn't get to it. In my defense, though, I had a story I needed to finish for the paper."

"Are you worried how the newspaper is going to run in your absence?" I asked.

"Oh, everything will be fine. My assistant editor is going to step up to the plate. She's pretty Type-A, so it probably means everything is going to run like a well-oiled machine."

"Perfect." And, honestly, it was nice to be with somebody who knew how to take a break. I wasn't completely sure that *I* did, and it would be nice to get some tips.

"You're sure Holly doesn't mind that I'm tagging along?" asked Grayson. "I mean, I haven't even met her. And we're staying a pretty long time."

"You're making her day, I promise. She's been fussing at me to find myself a boyfriend for years. Now she can pepper *you* with questions instead of giving me the third degree all the time. What time do you want to leave town tomorrow?"

Grayson said, "I feel like I should give you the opportunity to sleep in a little. You rarely get the chance, and it is your vacation."

I chuckled. "I forgot you don't know how uptight I am the night before a trip. My sleep is going to be pretty sketchy. Then, when I finally drift off, I'll be dreaming about packing. Or that we're in Charleston, and I've forgotten to pack something important."

"That stinks. So, no sleeping in?"

"It would probably be better if I tried to nod off in the car. If I'm not driving, I mean," I said.

"Oh, I can guarantee you that you won't be driving if you're wanting to nod off," said Grayson, a teasing note in his voice. "Okay, in that case, let's plan on leaving at seven. And bring a pillow and blanket. If you're going to sleep in the car, you might as well be comfortable."

And I was. The next morning, I was, unsurprisingly, awake at five. I got ready, ate breakfast, skipped my coffee, and then helped Grayson load my stuff, and Fitz, into the car.

From what Grayson told me later, Fitz and I both fell immediately to sleep. That's despite stop and go traffic on the road, a few sirens heading to an accident scene, and a tremendous storm he drove through.

Sometime later, I woke slowly up. It was very disorienting to find myself in a car, hurtling down the road at great speed. But it was lovely to find that several hours had magically elapsed, and that we were far closer to the historic port city than we'd been when I'd crashed into sleep.

"Did I snore?" I asked, yawning.

"No, but Fitz did," said Grayson with a grin. "I couldn't believe the amount of racket that one little cat could make."

"I guess he must have needed it. Do you want me to take over driving for a while? I'm definitely rested now. So rested that I'm not totally sure I'm going to fall asleep tonight."

Grayson said, "Sure, that would be great. Not about you having insomnia tonight, but that you're offering to drive. I could use a break."

He pulled us into a rest area where we took a short break. There were people walking dogs and hanging out at picnic tables. It felt good to stretch. Despite my pillow and blanket, I'd been curled into an awkward position. It was nice to straighten myself out again and work out the little cramps.

Grayson said, "Why don't we eat lunch before you start driving?"

I glanced around. "What, you mean grab something from those vending machines?" The thought wasn't very appealing, although I could certainly have downed a bag of Cheetos with no problem. Or maybe a Snickers bar. I'd apparently woken up with an appetite.

Grayson grinned at me, and I said, "Oh, wait. You were *organized*, weren't you?"

"You were pretty organized yourself with that packing! I didn't have as much stuff to wrap up yesterday at the newspaper as you did in the library. So, I took the liberty of putting together a small cooler." Which he quickly produced, to my delight.

I grabbed Fitz, still sleepy in his crate and stretching a bit as I carried him. We headed over to a shady area where there was a collection of picnic tables. There, we enjoyed mini charcuterie trays with meats, hummus, fruits, and veggies. Fitz had a snack, too, and watched with lazy interest from his carrier at the different dogs being walked around. The food was delicious, and mine disappeared quickly.

Soon we were back in the car, after giving Fitz a chance to use the litter box we'd brought. It was a beautiful day, and we had the sunroof open. Even though I thought I knew what we might expect from our trip, there was still this fun sense of adventure, expectation, and the mystery of what might really be in store.

Chapter Two

When we'd traveled quite a bit longer, we finally got into Charleston. We crossed the Ravenel Bridge with its delicate-looking web of cables and had our first glimpse of water.

"It's been forever since I've been to the beach," I said.

"Really? How long?"

I gave a wry smile. "Like over a decade? I was in college."

"Do you like the beach? Or are you more of a mountain person?" asked Grayson.

"I think I'm the kind of person who likes them both equally. Of course, I live in the mountains, so I see them all the time. But the beach always gives me much the same feeling. Looking at the ocean, like gazing over a mountain range, gave me a sense of infinity somehow." I glanced over at Grayson almost shy at my fancifulness.

But he was nodding in agreement. "I totally see what you're saying. It's almost like you get a sense of how small we all are and how vast nature is."

"Which is actually a really humbling thing. I enjoy realizing my everyday problems are fairly small and petty in the big picture."

As we drove into town, we were looking around us the whole time. The city, established in 1670, was like living history. The townhouses, the cobbled streets, the horse-drawn carriages filled with tourists, all gave the sense of a place that time forgot.

A few minutes later, we arrived at Holly's house. It was well-situated with proximity to downtown Charleston. The house had a wide front porch with a porch swing overlooking the front yard. Holly greeted us at the door with hugs and a very excited golden retriever named Murphy, who Holly had on a leash. She gave us a rueful look. "Murphy is totally thrilled that you're here. I'm going to keep him leashed until the excitement wears off."

Murphy grinned at us unrepentantly. Then his nose started twitching, and he curiously sniffed the air near Fitz's carrier.

Fitz gave an interested mew. He'd had some experience with dogs before, and had always kept being his normal, laid-back self. But we were in a totally new environment right now and around a completely different canine, so it made sense to take things slow.

"Here, let me help you in with your stuff. How was the trip here?"

We followed Holly upstairs, filling her in. In the process, Murphy grabbed a toy and flung it at our feet.

"Just ignore that," said Holly dryly. "He thinks you're here just to play with him."

"Your place is great," I said to Holly, looking around me. And it was. It was a sunny, plant-filled space with beautiful old furniture in nooks and crannies everywhere. "It looks just like you."

"Thanks! Lots of family furniture here. Plus, I love going antiquing on the weekends."

Holly gave us a short tour, and we took in the beautiful wooden floors, the soft rugs adorning them, and the cheerily painted walls.

"Why don't I take Murphy downstairs and let you get settled in for a few minutes? I bet Fitz wants to get out of his carrier
and explore a little?"

Grayson and I spent the next fifteen minutes unpacking our
stuff and Fitz's. I opened the door to his cat carrier, and he
padded out.

He looked solemnly around him, taking in the books, the
bed, and the bathroom. He made a lap around the upstairs, then
jumped on top of the quilt and happily rolled around, placing
himself in the exact location of a sunbeam.

Grayson chuckled. "I know I keep saying this, but that's the
most laid-back cat I've ever seen in my life."

"He's a good boy," I agreed, leaning over to scratch Fitz under his chin. He purred in agreement.

Grayson and I headed back downstairs where Murphy was
waiting in an agony of excitement, tail wagging so hard he was
sweeping the floor.

"Does Murphy like playing ball?" asked Grayson.

Murphy's ears pricked up at the word and his tongue lolled
out in a doggy grin.

Holly's eyes twinkled. "Oh, now you're in trouble. That's his
favorite thing in the world. But he's like a three-year-old . . . he
won't ever want to stop. You're the one who'll have to call it off."

"I could use the chance to stretch my legs a little after a long
day in the car. And it will give you and Ann the chance to catch
up."

Holly retrieved a disreputable-looking tennis ball from the
closet, and Grayson and Murphy headed into the fenced backyard. Murphy bounded as he went.

"He seems like a great guy, Ann," said Holly, a bit wistfully.

"Because he's entertaining Murphy?" I smiled at her.

Holly snorted. "Hey, that's a huge deal for me. Murphy has enough energy for three golden retrievers. Look how happy he is."

Sure enough, Murphy was bouncing around the backyard, doing an excellent impression of Tigger from Winnie-the-Pooh. His tail was wagging furiously, a delighted doggy grin on his face. Grayson looked happy and relaxed too, tossing the ball, and enjoying being outdoors.

Holly poured us both a glass of lemonade and asked a bunch of questions about Grayson, the library, and Fitz. Then I got caught up on how Holly was doing. She wasn't crazy about her job at a local bank, but she made a good living. She was still looking for someone special to go out with, but was tired enough at the end of the day that she often turned down friends' invitations to go out.

By the time Grayson and Murphy came back inside, we were laughing ourselves silly with stories from our college years.

Murphy headed right over to his water bowl, practically dunking his entire head into it in his efforts to get hydrated. Holly poured Grayson a glass of lemonade in the off-chance that he was even halfway as thirsty as the golden retriever was.

"Remembering the old days?" he asked with a grin.

Holly nodded, eyes twinkling. "How did you guess?"

"I think I know our mission during this trip then," said Grayson. "We need to create some new ones that are just as good. That way, you'll both have something to look back at and laugh about in another ten years."

"Oh, that's a great idea," said Holly. "Something to put on our to-do list. Which reminds me—what kinds of things do y'all want to do while you're here?"

"We're open to anything," Grayson and I responded in chorus. We both laughed.

Holly raised an eyebrow. "You're speaking in unison now? You really *are* a couple, aren't you?"

We were still sitting at Holly's kitchen table, chatting away, when Fitz loped curiously downstairs. He peeked around the wall to see what everyone was doing and to survey the sunbeam situation. Murphy's tail started drumming the floor ecstatically at the sight of the orange and white cat.

"Uh-oh. Looks like I better put his leash back on," said Holly.

I said, "Let's give him a minute and see what happens. Fitz can always retreat to higher ground if he needs to."

Fitz, seeing precisely the sunbeam he wanted to check out, padded over in our direction. Murphy, beside himself, started talking to Fitz in murmured yelps and chuffs. Fitz surveyed the dog seriously, coming closer. Murphy's eyes were wide at the unexpected closeness of the mysterious feline. Then Fitz apparently spotted something on Murphy's face that needed cleaning. He leaned in, licked the spot a few times while Murphy stood completely still. Then Fitz proceeded over to the sunbeam, where he started bathing himself.

"Extraordinary," breathed Holly.

Grayson shook his head. "Fitz gets along with everybody. And everything."

Fitz seemed to agree, a feline smile on his face.

It was sometime later, after we'd talked about plans for the week, and Holly and Grayson had gotten better acquainted when there was a knock at Holly's door. Murphy exploded into delighted barking, startling all of us except for Fitz. Fitz stared steadily at Murphy as if he'd totally been expecting that he was going to do that at any moment.

She frowned. "Okay. I don't get a lot of visitors here." Holly headed for the door, opening it cautiously. "Oh, Frank, it's you."

"Hey, Holly. I need to talk to you," a voice said.

Chapter Three

Holly opened the door wider and motioned into the house. "Come on in. You remember my college roommate, Ann, don't you?"

A man stepped inside, a few years older than Holly and me. He was a handsome man, tall and lean with a shock of blond hair. He was the kind of person who radiated energy. I could imagine it was usually directed toward whatever line of work he was in. But now, it seemed to pour out of him in a sort of nervous energy. I realized he looked vaguely familiar.

The man stopped short at the sight of Grayson and me. He hesitated. Then he said, "Oh, you've got company. Hey, Ann."

Suddenly, I could place him. It was Frank, Holly's older brother. I'd only met him a handful of times, and it had been many years earlier.

Holly said, "And this is Grayson Phillips, Ann's boyfriend. Grayson, this is my brother, Frank."

Grayson stepped forward and shook Frank's hand. "Good to meet you."

"Likewise," said Frank, rather absently. He hesitated again, as if wanting to say something but not wanting to at the same time.

"Is everything okay?" asked Holly. "You don't drop by very often."

"No, I guess I don't. I probably should, though. Yes, everything is fine. I was just in the neighborhood and thought I'd stop by."

"Want to come in and have a seat for a while? I've got fresh lemonade," said Holly.

Frank gave her a tight smile. "Usually, I'd like that, but I'm actually on a bit of a schedule."

It struck me as an odd thing to say, especially considering the fact that he'd chosen to stop by Holly's house, something which was apparently out of the ordinary.

"I should go," said Frank. "Maybe call me later on, Holly? Good to meet you, Grayson, and to see you again, Ann."

With that, he left just as abruptly as he'd arrived.

Holly frowned at the closed door. "That was kind of weird."

I shook my head. "It sounds like he came over to bounce something off of you and then was thrown because Grayson and I were here. Sorry, we should have offered to give you some privacy."

Holly shrugged, walking back over to the kitchen table and sitting down. "Frank's never bounced anything off me before. He's always looked at me like I'm still six years old and he's the big brother who can handle everything." She paused and snorted. "He actually *is* the big brother who can handle everything. I'm the one who asks his opinion about everything. He was totally involved when I bought this house."

Grayson asked, "What does Frank do?"

"He's a dentist," said Holly. "A pretty good one, too. He and a partner own his practice, which is in a great location. Frank's recently gone through a divorce, so that was tough on him. But he's so busy between his work and his hobby that I don't even know how much the divorce registered with him."

"Hobby?" I asked.

"More than a hobby, actually. Sort of a passion of his. He's a relic hunter."

Grayson and I just stared at Holly. Of all the potential hobbies she could have mentioned, relic hunting was the last one I'd have expected.

Holly chuckled. "If you could see the expressions on your faces. I promise it's not uncommon here in Charleston. The city is in a period of tremendous growth, which is in direct conflict with the need to protect and preserve artifacts. Often companies will actually pay relic hunters to explore sites before they build homes or businesses."

"And Frank has found things at sites?" asked Grayson.

Holly nodded. "A veritable treasure trove from both the American Revolution and the Civil War. Anyway, enough about my brother. What do you feel like doing? Want any food?"

"Grayson packed us lunch for the road, but I have to admit I'm feeling a little hungry still," I said.

Holly nodded. "Are you okay with getting back in the car after so many hours of driving? I was thinking maybe we could drive over to take a walk on Rainbow Row—stretch your legs a little. Then, after we've worked up more of an appetite, we could grab something to eat. Charleston has tons of really acclaimed restaurants."

"Sounds perfect!" Once again, Grayson and I were both in chorus.

Holly laughed. "Y'all are just too cute."

Holly drove us over to Tradd Street where we parked and set off on a walk along the waterfront. Rainbow Row, a Charleston landmark, comprised thirteen pastel-colored homes dating back to the mid-1700s. We took pictures, chatted, and enjoyed getting a little exercise. We followed this up with a sumptuous meal at a restaurant nearby. Naturally, Grayson and I had to order shrimp and grits. It was just too tempting to pass up. Usually, I ordered the cheapest thing on the menu whenever we went out to eat, but this vacation was an opportunity for me to splurge for once.

When we got home, Holly made us mixed drinks, and we sat outside in her fenced yard with Murphy and Fitz. The two animals had appeared to make friends; at least, Murphy seemed to have given up on the idea of trying to get Fitz to play with him. Fitz curled up in my lap as we all chatted, drank, and laughed until it was far past the time I usually turned in.

The following morning, the sun streaming through the window made me realize I'd slept much longer than usual. My first reaction was one of panic, as if I'd overslept for work. Fitz, who was curled up against my chest, opened an alarmed eye as if sensing I was about to bolt out of bed.

A few minutes later, though, Fitz gave me a somber look. The kind of look that means he's really very hungry and is rather disappointed that there's nothing currently in his bowl. I slipped out of bed as quietly as I could.

I opened a can of cat food, giving Fitz half. He happily gulped it down while I headed into the bathroom to get showered and ready for the day. By the time I was done, I could hear voices downstairs. Fitz padded behind me as I opened the door and headed down toward them.

Grayson and Holly were in the kitchen, drinking coffee and eating eggs and toast. Murphy grinned at me, although most of his attention was focused on the food on the table above his head.

"Hey there!" said Grayson, smiling at me.

"Hey to you," I said, smiling back.

"Too cute," murmured Holly under her breath. Then she said, "Ready for some coffee and breakfast?"

"You're my hero," I said ruefully. "I think I may have over-served myself last night. But it sure was fun."

Grayson said, "I'm going to hit the shower. Thanks for breakfast, Holly." He put his plate in the dishwasher and headed upstairs with his coffee.

An hour later, we'd decided to go to King Street and do a little walking and shopping on the historic street, which was lined by palmetto trees. Some buildings were hundreds of years old, which was, in America at least, a heady idea. I wanted to be an overachiever and get started with some Christmas presents. Neither Grayson nor I had a lot of extra spending money for major shopping, but it was fun to window shop and buy small things. There were tons of specialty shops for local chocolates, artisanal cheeses, and curated wine. There were plenty of antique shops, too, which Holly enjoyed sticking her head into. She showed us around some of her favorite shops. I loved the look of antiques, even if I didn't have the budget for them.

We'd spent a little over an hour browsing through shops and people watching when Holly's phone rang. She frowned. "Hello? Yes, this is Holly Walsh."

Grayson and I stopped walking, as Holly froze. "Sorry, what? No, I'm not at home, I'm downtown. What's this about?

No, I don't want to meet you. I want you to tell me right now what's going on."

Holly swayed a little, and Grayson grabbed her arm.

"No," she said in a pained voice. "No, you've got to be wrong. I just saw him." She took a deep breath. "Not this morning, no. Last night. Where are you now? I'll be right there."

Holly's face was pale underneath her tan.

"Holly, who was that? What's wrong?" I asked.

Holly shook her head and then burst into tears. Grayson and I steered her into a clothing store where there was a place for her to sit down.

"It's Frank," she sobbed. "He's dead."

Chapter Four

A police officer had been the person on the phone. They'd looked up her number on Frank's phone and an officer had been sent over to Holly's house to inform her.

"Can we go over to where Frank is?" Holly asked us.

"Of course," said Grayson quickly.

"Did the police tell you where he was?"

Holly nodded, standing up and seeming steadier. "At the downtown branch of the library. So not far from here." She gave a short laugh. "They didn't want me to come over. Apparently, it's a crime scene."

Grayson and I exchanged a glance. It didn't make much sense that a dentist would be murdered in a library. Hoping to get some more answers when we arrived, we hurried with Holly to the car. I offered to drive, and Holly quickly took me up on it. She was really in no shape to drive a car.

Minutes later, we were at the main branch of the library. There was a police presence outside and two policemen barred our entry.

Holly wasn't having any of it, though. "I'm his sister," she said in a fierce voice. "They said I could come over."

From what I'd understood on the way over, that was a fib. I was sure the last thing the police wanted was for their crime scene to be compromised.

The policemen also seemed doubtful. One of them walked a few steps away and spoke on his radio. Turning back around, he said, "I'm afraid we can't let you inside. We have a team in there collecting evidence. But one of the detectives is coming down to speak with you."

The sun was blazing down, and the concrete wasn't helping. The policeman continued, "Why don't you sit over there? There are a couple of benches, and it's in the shade."

We gave him a grateful smile and headed over to the benches.

Holly sank down on a bench and held her head in her hands. "I can't believe this is happening. We just saw Frank last night! Everything was fine."

I wondered about this. Yes, Frank was in perfect health last night, from what we could see. But it was also obvious that something was on his mind. He'd seemed very tense. Worried.

"Did the police indicate what might have happened?" I asked.

Holly shook her head. We waited silently a few minutes until a suited tall man with short-clipped dark hair conferred with the police officers at the door and then approached us.

"Holly Walsh?" he asked quietly.

Holly nodded.

"I'm Lieutenant Aaron Roberts. I'm so sorry about your brother."

"It's true then?" Holly's eyes filled with tears. She'd obviously been holding onto hope that perhaps a terrible mistake had been made. Misidentification of some kind.

"I'm afraid so. A librarian discovered your brother in the research area of the library about an hour before we contacted you."

Holly's voice trembled. "He was dead there? Or did he die in an ambulance?"

"Unfortunately, he was already deceased by the time the librarian found him." He paused. "Do you know anything about why your brother might have been at the library?"

Holly said slowly, "Only vaguely. He'd have been conducting research, I'm sure."

"Was he often in the library doing research?" asked Roberts.

"Yes. He was a relic hunter in his spare time. He spent a good deal of time in the library looking up historical information on various sites and poring over the Sanborn maps."

Roberts took out a small notepad and pen and jotted down a few notes. "Did you speak with Frank recently?"

"Just last night," said Holly, glancing at Grayson and me. "My friends are visiting Charleston and staying at my place. Frank dropped by unexpectedly last night, saying he wanted to talk to me."

"Was that unusual?"

Holly said, "Yes, it was. We chatted from time to time, but he wasn't the kind of guy to sit down and have deep, important conversations with me. It seemed like he had something on his mind, but he didn't stick around. Then, when I tried to call him later, he didn't answer his phone." She looked startled. "He wasn't dead last night, was he?"

I could tell the idea that her brother's body had somehow been overlooked at the library the previous night was disturbing to her.

"No. His time of death is going to be determined more firmly later, but we suspect it's around 9:30 this morning. He died shortly before the librarian discovered him there." Roberts paused. "Do you have any idea who might have wished him harm?"

"It's definitely a suspicious death, then?" Holly's voice cracked a bit as she asked the question, and I gave her hand a squeeze. She squeezed it back, gratefully.

He nodded tersely. "I'm afraid so."

Holly took a deep breath. "I'm not totally sure." She paused, thinking. "Frank was recently divorced."

Roberts made a note of this. "Could you tell me a little about that?"

Holly quickly said, "I'm not saying that June had anything to do with it. I mean, why would she? Her relationship with Frank was over, and she was moving on."

Roberts asked, "Her name is June?"

Holly said, "June Walsh." She gave Roberts her contact information.

Roberts said, "You mentioned June was moving on. Does that mean she's engaged in another relationship?"

Holly hesitated for a moment. Then she said, "She's actually in a relationship with the mayor."

Roberts' pen stopped moving on the notepad, and he regarded Holly with interest. "Is that so? How long had that relationship been going on?"

"According to Frank, their marriage was over before June's relationship with Paul started. But hey—like I was saying, that doesn't mean that June is involved in this. It doesn't make any sense for her to. They were divorced, and June was free to see whomever she wanted."

"Can you think of anyone else who might have been upset with your brother?"

Holly shook her head. "There might be something I'm forgetting, but I just can't think right now. Can I get back to you later? After I get my head together?"

Roberts nodded. "Of course. I'm sorry for your loss. Here's my card, in case you remember anything later on or have any questions." He handed her his business card, then glanced away toward the library. "If you'll excuse me?"

As he walked away, I noticed there were a group of people standing right outside the library. One of them was looking our way. They looked to me like librarians—dressed in business casual, they didn't look like patrons. The woman who'd been looking our way started walking over.

"Can we get out of here?" muttered Holly.

"Sure," I said. "But it looks like someone is coming over to speak with you. Are you up to it? She might be a library employee."

Holly nodded and stood up as the woman came closer.

Chapter Five

"I'm sorry," said the woman. "I'm Meredith, and I'm one of the librarians here. I couldn't help but notice the detective was speaking with you."

Holly said, "My brother was the victim here." Her voice shook again, but she regained control of it by the end of the sentence.

"I'm sorry," said Meredith again, her voice softer. "What a terrible thing to happen."

"Were you there?" asked Holly.

Meredith nodded. "I'm a research librarian, so I'm often in that area of the library . . . the South Carolina room. I saw your brother in the Charleston Archive quite a bit. We'd chat sometimes. I know he was a relic hunter." She glanced over at a man who was standing in front of the library with a lost expression on his face. "That gentleman over there is often here, too. I think he and your brother were friends, or at least they worked on research together sometimes."

The man was a reedy-looking guy, young, with narrow eyes. He was looking in our direction with interest.

Holly said, "Can you tell me what happened? The police weren't able to tell me very much, but they said it wasn't an accident."

"I'm afraid that's correct," said Meredith. She seemed to try to choose her words carefully. "One of our bookshelves in the research area was toppled on him. I'm so sorry."

Holly stared at her. "A bookshelf?"

"It would have been very heavy. And there's no way it would have come down on its own."

Holly frowned. "But wouldn't that have made a tremendous crash? Wouldn't you see whoever did it?"

Meredith said, "I was actually on another floor, finding some materials for a patron. Someone heard the crash downstairs, but by the time they could get to the research room, the perpetrator was already gone."

"Were there any cameras?" I asked.

"Not inside the library, no. There is footage for outside, so we're going to provide it for the police, of course. Unfortunately, I don't think the quality of the tape will be great. But maybe they'll be able to get some sort of information from the video."

Holly shook her head. "I just can't believe this is happening."

I cleared my throat. "Meredith, it sounds like you were pretty well acquainted with Frank. Do you know what he was working on?"

"I do, actually. He asked me for help once to locate some information. He was studying the Sanborn maps."

Grayson said, "I'm sorry—I don't know anything about those. Are they historic maps?"

Meredith nodded. "There are quite a few of them. Sanborn was a fire insurance company. We have some of their maps from 1888. As you can imagine, they provide information on what was in a particular city location long ago. Researchers can determine who was living there at the time and often locate more information."

Grayson said, "Do you think one of Frank's relic hunting projects could have resulted in his murder?"

Meredith held up her hands. "I have no idea. It's a possibility, though." Grayson was still frowning, so she explained, "So, businesses will buy sites and will want to do their due diligence to make sure they're not building over historic artifacts. They'll call in these relic hunters. Most of the time, these folks are hobbyists."

"They're not being paid?" I asked.

"Usually not. But often, they're allowed to keep whatever they find. Then those items go into their private collections or they might sell them to other collectors. It's also a pretty competitive field." Meredith glanced over again at the young man near the library entrance. "That guy I mentioned earlier is one of your brother's competitors."

Grayson said slowly, "So why might someone be killed over relic hunting?"

"Well, it could be the competitor felt he or she got edged out—like it should have been their site to explore. Or maybe the business wanted to shut down the research," said Meredith.

I said, "Because what's found could endanger their construction?"

"Exactly. Sometimes relic hunters don't just find pottery or old coins or belt buckles or weapons. Sometimes they might stumble across human remains. And that would shut down any type of construction, sometimes for good. If a business thought they'd lose their investment, that could be reason enough for murder." Meredith glanced at her watch. "I'd better go. I need to find our director and see what our next steps are. Again, I'm so sorry about what happened."

"Thanks so much for coming over to speak with us," said Holly, giving Meredith a smile.

We watched as Meredith walked away. As she drew closer to the group of librarians, I saw the young man she'd mentioned quickly speak to her. Meredith looked our way and then said a few words. He nodded and walked in our direction.

"Holly," I said, "Are you up for this? Or would you rather go back to your place?"

Holly shook her head. "I'd rather see if we can get more information about what happened, first. Maybe it'll be easier for me to wrap my head around if I can learn a little more."

The reedy-looking young man came up to us in an apologetic matter. His thin fingers were clutching a battered briefcase. When he gave us a nervous smile, we could see he was wearing braces on his teeth.

"Hi," he said awkwardly. "I'm Warner Andrews. I was just speaking with Meredith, and she mentioned that you're Frank's family."

Holly nodded. "I'm Frank's sister, Holly. These are my friends who are staying with me right now—Ann and Grayson."

Warner greeted us somberly, carefully shaking our hands with the hand that wasn't holding his briefcase. "I wanted to let you know how sorry I was about this. I can't believe that something like this would happen in the library."

Holly gave him a weak smile. "Thank you. I understand you were a friend of Frank's?"

Warner looked a little at a loss for words. I got the impression that he and Frank hadn't exactly been friends. He finally said, "We were colleagues. Frank and I are both relic hunters." He peered at us. "You know about relic hunters?"

Holly said, "A little. My friends are hearing more about it for the first time." She paused. "Were you in the library with him? When it happened?"

Warner looked a bit shocked at this. "No, I wasn't with him. If I had been, I'm guessing this would never have happened."

"You know what happened, though?" asked Holly.

Warner shook his head. "Not more than you do. I was out in the field sifting through a site when this happened, apparently. I arrived at the library not long ago and found the entrance taped off with crime scene tape. One of the other librarians, not Meredith, filled me in. I can't believe somebody would do something like that."

Holly said, "Who do you think did this? Since you know him pretty well."

Warner looked uncomfortable. "I was thinking it was some sort of random act of violence. A malicious act by somebody who just wasn't totally right in the head."

Holly was already shaking her head while Warner was talking. "No way. I don't believe that. When I was talking to Meredith, she was thinking it might have something to do with the research Frank was working on."

Warner now looked even more uncomfortable. "I don't really know much about what he was working on."

"Did you sometimes work at the same site together?" I asked.

Warner directed his attention to me, looking solemnly at me. "Not really. I mean, sometimes Frank and I consulted with each other."

"Were you more like rivals, then?" asked Holly, obviously thinking back to what Meredith was saying.

"Competitors," said Warner quickly. "Friendly competitors."

"Friendly all the time?" asked Holly in a doubtful voice. "I'm just asking because I've always thought Frank was ambitious. He always wanted to have a better report card than me."

"And did he?" asked Warner, sounding curious.

"Naturally," said Holly, wryly. "But he was always driven." She suddenly burst into tears.

Warner now was even more uncomfortable than he'd seemed earlier. He reached out to pat Holly awkwardly on the arm. "Frank and I had our differences sometimes, but he was a great guy. Smart as a whip. And, yeah, he could be really competitive, but that's what made him such a successful relic hunter."

Holly continued crying, and Warner looked to me for help. Grayson was also looking at me as if he wished he could escape. I put my arm around Holly and fished out some tissues from my purse. To distract Warner and give Holly time to get her emotions under control again, I said, "Tell us a little more about the work you and Frank were doing. What kinds of things have you found?"

Warner and Grayson looked relieved by the change of subject. "Well, we've found all sorts of things. We look at old maps and various historical documents to help us find good places to dig."

Grayson asked, "So you don't just work at construction sites?"

"No. I mean, we get plenty of business digging for businesses who want to make sure they're not covering up a historic site. But we also go to areas that were old settlements or trade routes. We're very careful, of course, with our approach."

I asked, "Wouldn't most of the property you work on be privately owned, these days?"

Warner nodded. "It is. But usually, the property owners are interested, too. Or, if they're not, they're happy to have us pay for exploring the property."

"And I suppose you're not just digging randomly—the maps are helping you pinpoint the location better," said Grayson.

"That's right. Although sometimes there is an element of random digging. Naturally, we're also using tools like metal detectors. Frank and I always made sure we were doing historically responsible digging."

Grayson asked, "What happens when you find something valuable on the property owner's site?"

"Well, it depends on whatever deal you agree on in advance. Sometimes, whatever we find is ours to keep. Sometimes, especially if it's something really interesting and valuable, the homeowner might want a percentage of the profits after you sell the piece to collectors." Warner looked at me. "But to answer your question, we find all sorts of things. Military gear, bullets, farming equipment, buttons, all sorts of things."

Grayson asked, "What do you do with the artifacts you find?"

"And what did Frank do?" added Holly.

Warner puffed up a little, feeling important at the attention. "Museums purchase many of the relics for their collections. But sometimes we keep some of them for ourselves. Frank liked to go around to different clubs and schools and stuff and talk about his personal collection." Warner shrugged as if speaking in public wasn't exactly his thing.

Holly asked, "Were you planning on meeting Frank here? I mean, is that why you're at the library?"

Warner quickly shook his head. "Nope. I didn't know Frank was here today. I mean, he had a pretty busy schedule. Sometimes he was at his dental practice."

"Did he have certain days or times that he was usually here?" I asked.

Warner said, "Nothing that organized, no. But things could come up, you know, especially with his job. Sometimes he'd *plan* on being at the library, but he'd have to go into work unexpectedly because somebody had a dental emergency. I was just here to hunt through some maps and try to figure out my next site. I was running late today because I overslept."

I was curious about what type of work Warner did for his day job. Whatever it was, it must be the kind of thing that allowed him some flexibility. "Were you up late working last night?"

Warner chuckled. "No. Actually, I'm between jobs right now. I'm in IT and I need to find something that's going to allow me to follow my passion. Which, clearly, is relic hunting and not IT. I was up late last night playing video games."

Grayson said, "Oh, you're a gamer. What do you like to play?"

I knew Grayson was far from being a gamer, but he had a couple of friends who were really into it. He'd play with them sometimes and usually was killed in the first twenty minutes.

Warner looked at Grayson as if he could tell he wasn't seriously into games. He shrugged. "RPG, RTS, FPS. How about you?"

"Same," said Grayson, although he looked like he wasn't completely sure what those types of gaming were.

"Gaming is a great stress reliever," said Warner. "It's just so totally absorbing. It helps you forget things. I've got online friends I'll play with or against, which makes it more interesting. Anyway, I totally lost track of the time." He hazarded a look at Holly, as if to make sure she'd stopped crying. "It's a good way to escape."

Knowing Holly, I had the feeling her escape routes didn't involve video games. But she nodded.

Warner cleared his throat. "For Frank, his escape was relic hunting. Don't get me wrong; he was a great dentist. I heard people talk about him all the time. But that was just his day job. It wasn't exciting to him at all. This was what he loved to do. And he'd had a big find lately. Did he tell you about that?"

Holly shook her head. "We didn't really talk much about his relic hunting."

"He'd found some Spanish pirate booty. Not a lot, but some. Pre-US Revolution." Warner's eyes were envious. "It was a significant find."

"I wish I'd talked more with him about this stuff," muttered Holly. She paused. Then she said, "I know you said you thought this might be just random violence, but I don't think it is. Can you think of people who might have been upset with my brother?"

Warner considered this, looking down at his orange tennis shoes. "I don't know. I mean, I don't want to get anybody into trouble, or anything. But Frank and I would chat sometimes when we were working on a site together."

"I thought you and he were more like competitors," said Grayson.

"Sure, we were. But we'd also end up on the same site sometimes, during a group dig. Anyway, the work could be tedious. I kind of *love* tedious. But we'd talk some during those times. Frank had a lot to say about Carl Hopkins."

Grayson and I glanced at Holly, not recognizing the name.

Holly said, "Carl is my brother's partner at the dental practice. But I always thought they got along fine. They weren't really friends or anything; they weren't going to hang out after work. But they had a solid, professional relationship. Frank always said that he respected Carl and that he was a great dentist. He was older than Frank and was a kind of mentor when Frank first joined the practice."

Warner shrugged. "I don't know about that. All I know is that there was a big issue that didn't look like it was going to be easily resolved."

I was getting irritated with Warner. He seemed like the kind of person who liked to *know* information and then felt smug when he was the only one who did. I said a bit curtly, "What issue was that?"

Warner looked a bit surprised by my tone. "Well, Carl wanted to sell the practice. Frank was holding out. It was pretty amazing that Frank was an owner in the practice anyway, considering how young he was."

Holly didn't say anything, just held Warner's gaze. I knew that Holly's family was very well-off, which was most likely why Holly had such a great house and why Frank owned part of the practice where he worked.

Warner apparently realized he wasn't going to get any additional information. He looked a bit disappointed. Then he said with a bit of spite, "I bet Carl is going to be delighted that he can do what he wanted to with the property, with Frank gone. It's taken care of a bunch of problems for him. I'm not saying he did anything to Frank, you know. Just that his death is going to work out pretty well for him."

Holly stared at him for a few moments. "Why did Carl want to leave the practice? Was he thinking about moving it to a different location? Did he get a great offer?"

"Let me think for a minute so I can remember."

I was about to get irritated again, but Warner appeared to be trying to excavate the information from the far reaches of his brain, so I didn't say anything this time.

Warner wagged his finger, looking relieved. "Got it. Carl needed to move closer to his mom. She's not doing well and needs some help."

"Okay. Then why not just allow the practice to continue and have a new dentist take his spot?" asked Grayson.

"Apparently, Carl needed the money. I guess he was worried about his parents needing more care? Anyway, he wanted to sell the practice and the property instead of having to worry about being a remote landlord and leasing it to renters. Frank was especially mad about one thing—without telling him, Carl had found some interested buyers who wanted the whole thing."

Holly said thoughtfully, "But Frank didn't want to sell."

"Right. He was in a different stage of life. He liked the location and didn't want to have to find a new place to practice. Plus, he told me he thought there might be all kinds of tax ramifications and liabilities with the sale of the practice building plus the property. He said Carl was putting more and more pressure on him."

Holly frowned. "You think Carl could have gotten frustrated with him and just decided to get rid of him?"

Warner held up his hands defensively. "Hey, like I said, I don't know anything. I'm just telling you what Frank told me. I don't even know Carl. I have no idea what he might or might not be capable of." He sighed. "I'd better get going. Sorry again about your brother, Holly. It was good meeting all of you."

And with that, he was gone.

Chapter Six

I looked over at Holly. She seemed completely exhausted. "Want to go back home?" I asked her.

She said quietly, "I'm not sure what I want right now. I realize I need to call my parents and let them know what happened. But this is going to be so devastating to them. They were crazy about Frank and were always so proud of him. I probably need to let the extended family know, too, because I'm sure my folks won't be up to it. But I'm not sure I'm totally up to the task right now. I hate to be the one to break the bad news to them, but I know it'll be better coming from me."

"There's no reason you have to tell them right this second," I said.

Grayson shifted uncomfortably. "This is going to be a tough time for you, Holly. Ann and I really appreciate the great hospitality you've shown us. But maybe it would be best for us to move to a hotel for the rest of our stay. Especially since you're going to have family coming in for a service."

Holly quickly said, "No, please, stay with me. It's the perfect distraction. My folks won't want to stay with me . . . they always go to a fancy hotel when they visit Charleston. I know you'll understand if I end up leaving y'all up to your own devices sometimes, though. I'll make sure you have a key so you can come and go when I'm not available."

"Absolutely," I said. "And we can give you a hand with anything you need help with, too."

Holly glanced behind me. "Looks like Meredith is coming back over to have another word with us."

The librarian joined us with an apologetic air. "Sorry. It's just that I wanted to say a little more about Warner. I noticed you were talking with him for a while."

"He had a lot to say," said Holly, a little ruefully.

Meredith nodded. "Warner's in the library a lot, as I think I mentioned before. He even asked me out one time. I thought he was a nice enough guy and ended up going out with him for a coffee." She paused. "While we were at the coffee, I brought up Frank. Just casually. Like I said, I knew they were colleagues of a sort, and Frank was in the library even more than Warner was. Warner's entire attitude changed then."

"Because you mentioned Frank? How did he change?"

Meredith said, "I could tell he was really bitter about Frank's success. He said he thought Frank used his connections to poach sites that Warner thought should have been his. He was talking about it like Frank was almost cheating somehow."

I thought again about Holly's family. Not only did they have money, I knew they were well-connected, too. Holly and Frank had grown up in Charleston and hung out with other influential families. Although their parents had moved away, they'd chosen to stay and probably still nurtured many of those relationships. I could imagine that someone like Warner might get annoyed at Frank using his network to relic hunt.

Meredith continued, "Anyway, Warner was clearly pretty angry, and I decided I didn't want that kind of energy around me. Also, he had me pay for both our coffees. He was kind of apologetic about it, but he wasn't working at the time."

"It sounds like he still doesn't have a day job," said Holly.

Meredith said, "Makes sense. He's always at the library at odd times." She grimaced. "I'm not saying that Warner did anything. He seems pretty harmless. But I wanted to let you know, just in case. And of course, I'm going to tell the detective that Warner may not have been Frank's biggest fan. That little episode just occurred to me."

"Thanks for letting the detective know," said Holly.

We started walking to the car as Meredith headed back toward the library. I was feeling unsure about what we should do next. I didn't know if Holly would prefer to spend some time alone or if she wanted to have Grayson and me around for a while as a distraction. Finally, I asked her.

Holly mulled this over for a few seconds. She said, "You know, I think I'll feel better if I just go home, stare at the wall for a while, and snuggle with Murphy. Maybe cry a little. Do you mind if I send you two out to explore on your own?"

"Not a bit," I said.

"We totally understand," agreed Grayson.

We had a quiet ride back to Holly's house, each of us in our own thoughts. When we pulled up to Holly's place, it was almost as if Murphy had a sixth sense about Holly's emotional state—he was looking anxiously out the window and started making small barks when he spotted her. Fitz then appeared in another window, sitting on the sill and looking curiously out at the driveway.

Holly gave us a smile. "There's nothing quite like a dog waiting for you. Or, I guess, a cat." She glanced up at the sky and said, "You know, today might be the perfect day for you to head to the beach. It's sunny, not too humid. There's sure to be a nice breeze near the ocean. A day like this is a blessing this time of the year."

I looked over at Grayson and he gave me a thumbs-up. Holly was right. Considering everything that was going through my head right then, I didn't believe I could go sightsee and genuinely take anything in. The beach sounded like the perfect idea.

Grayson and I went inside to change and put together a bag of waters, sunscreen, and other stuff for the beach. I also wanted to check on Fitz and make sure he was doing all right, although I'd seen him in the window. After all, he was in a totally different location with different smells—and a dog. When we got inside, though, Fitz had already jumped down from the windowsill and was sprawled out on the floor downstairs in a sunbeam. I figured he must have vacated the spot only when he wanted to see what Murphy was barking at. He lazily opened an eye and started purring as we approached.

"I guess Murphy and Fitz are friends now," said Holly, a bit of wonder in her voice. "I never would have thought a cat would want to hang out in the same room as Murphy."

"Fitz is a pretty extraordinary cat," said Grayson, shaking his head and looking at Fitz admiringly. Murphy was flinging toys at Grayson's feet, not far from the orange and white cat, and Fitz was completely unfazed. What's more, it even looked as if Fitz was toying with the idea of participating in some sort of game with the dog.

Holly walked into the kitchen to fix herself a cup of hot tea. Grayson and I got ready to head back out again. I said, "Holly,

I've got my phone and a portable charger. Please let me know if you need us to head back or if you need anything at all."

Grayson said, "We can run errands for you on the way home, too. Whatever you need."

Holly's eyes glistened. "Thanks, y'all. I appreciate it. I'm going to be fine, though. I just need a little time to process everything." Then, apparently wanting to change the subject, she started talking about the beach. "Folly Beach is the closest, although there are others. You could also head out to Sullivan's Island or Isle of Palms."

"Which one do you recommend?" I asked.

"It's sort of whatever you're in the mood for. Sullivan's will probably be the quietest. Isle of Palms will have plenty of activity. And Folly is good for people-watching and quirkiness."

Grayson and I looked at each other. "Folly?" I asked him. Grayson nodded.

Holly said, "It's a really funky, low-key spot. I think you'll enjoy it. Be sure to grab something to eat at one of the restaurants there."

It wasn't long before we were at the beach. Holly had warned us that parking could be tricky, but fortunately, it wasn't that bad. We were probably lucking out because it was in the middle of a workday.

We opened the trunk, where we'd thrown the beach gear. Grayson chuckled. "I don't think we packed enough stuff."

I grinned at him. "It looks like we're planning on living on the beach." I grew more serious. "I just couldn't think, you know? I felt so bad for Holly. So I just kept grabbing things. We probably have three bottles of sunscreen."

"I was the same way." Grayson frowned. "Come to think of it, let me take a look at what we have."

After a quick inventory, Grayson came to the conclusion that not only did we have far too many extras of some items (sunscreen and towels), but we had forgotten other things we'd planned on bringing (water).

"Yeah, we're going to need water," I said, making a face. "I hate to lose our parking spot, though."

"There were plenty of them," said Grayson with a shrug. "How about if you get some of our stuff set up on the beach, and I run to the store real quick? I'll be back in a jiffy."

We checked our GPS and saw that the closest spot was Bert's Market. Grayson drove off and I headed down to the beach with a couple of towels and a bag of assorted other stuff.

The tide still seemed to be coming in, and the ocean had lots of rolling waves. There were surfers with varying degrees of expertise who were trying to ride them. I lay back on the towel and put my sunglasses on.

"I can tell you were worried that I took so long," said Grayson in a teasing voice.

I blinked behind my sunglasses. "What? Did I fall asleep?"

"You were out cold. There was a seagull right next to you, looking like he was about to rummage through your beach bag."

I yawned. "No food in there."

Grayson said, a note of pride in his voice. "Not yet. But Bert's had sandwiches for sale, so I bought some."

I sat up, still feeling drowsy. "I can't believe I just passed out on the beach like that. I don't usually take naps."

"Maybe due to the fact that it was such an unsettling morning," suggested Grayson.

I glanced at my watch and saw that it had indeed taken a while for Grayson to return to the beach. "Have a tough time finding parking?"

He grimaced. "You could say that. I had to drive around the block a few times. But eventually, a surfer finished loading his surfboard and drove away, and I took her spot." He handed me a water.

For a few minutes, we sat quietly, watching the surfers navigating the waves and a couple of small children playing with buckets in the shallows. Then Grayson asked, "Did you know Frank very well?"

I shook my head. "No. He came to the school once on family weekend, I think. And he helped Holly a couple of times when we were moving in or out of the dorm. But I never got the impression that he and Holly were very close. He was older than she was."

"What do you make of what happened last night?" asked Grayson. "When Frank showed up at Holly's door, I figured he wasn't in the mood to socialize with you and me, and that's why he took off."

I took a sip of my water, thinking. "I was wondering at the time if he had something personal that he wanted to bounce off Holly. Maybe something to do with his divorce. But now I wonder if it was something else. Like maybe he was worried about something."

Grayson nodded. "You think it had something to do with his relic hunting?"

"It might have. He definitely had something on his mind. But maybe it had something to do with his practice and him not wanting to sell it although his partner did. Whatever it was, I guess it was something that he wanted to confide in Holly about."

Grayson stretched out on his towel and put his sunglasses on. I did the same thing. We were quiet for another few moments before Grayson said, "That guy Warner, the other relic hunter, was sort of offbeat, wasn't he?"

"Awkward, for sure."

Grayson said, "I can kind of understand where he's coming from, though. From what he said, he and Frank were basically competitors. And Meredith, the librarian, was saying that he was upset with Frank for using his connections to get the best relic hunting sites." He turned his head and glanced over at me. "How did a dentist end up being so well-connected?"

"Remembering back from when I was in college, Holly's parents were bigwigs of some kind. To me, of course, they were just parents, but I realized there was a good deal of money there. Plus, they were both very involved in Charleston politics, from what I recall. Holly would roll her eyes a little. Sometimes, when she was home from college, she'd had to go to political fundraisers that she thought were really boring. I can't remember what her parents did . . . maybe work on the council?" I shrugged.

"But they're not local anymore? Holly mentioned them staying in a fancy hotel when they got here."

I said, "No, they moved to Virginia for her dad's work. I'm honestly not sure what he does. I think he's a CEO of something." I gave Grayson a wry smile. "Clearly, I wasn't all that interested in Holly's family when I was at school."

"Well, it was college. I mean, I wasn't exactly spending my time thinking about my roommate's family, either. I was either studying or trying to find out where the next weekend's party was going to be."

I had to chuckle at this. Grayson didn't exactly fit my image of a partier. "Really?"

"Sure," he grinned at me. "I went to a small school in an even smaller town. There wasn't a lot to do. Luckily for me, I managed to graduate with an English degree without too much trouble, but that was mostly just because I enjoyed reading."

"Did you always want to be a journalist?" I asked.

He chuckled. "Nope. If I had, I'd have at least applied to one of the big journalism schools. I just knew I was good at English. My parents were a little worried about what I planned on doing with that degree."

"What was their suggestion?" I asked with a smile. "Although I have a feeling I know what it might have been."

"Law school, of course." He grinned at me. "That's apparently the only right answer when one is an English major."

"But that didn't have any appeal for you?" I was pretty sure of his answer again. I couldn't picture easy going Grayson as a lawyer.

He shook his head. "The whole idea was the total opposite of what I wanted. I did consider becoming an English teacher, though. Maybe for high school."

I rolled over to get the sun on my back. "You'd have been a great teacher, actually. Probably would have converted a bunch of kids into English majors. But you're great as a newspaper editor, too."

"I just kind of fell into it," he said with a shrug.

We were quiet for a few minutes before he sighed. "I just feel awful for Holly. I know she said she wants us to stay over with her, but are you sure we shouldn't move to a hotel? Her family is going to be in and out, surely, and I don't want to be in their way. Or be any trouble for Holly, who seems great."

I shook my head. "Holly never says anything she doesn't mean. She wasn't just telling us to stay to be nice—I think she genuinely wants us there to be a distraction for her."

"Got it," said Grayson. "Well, maybe we can pick up supper tonight and bring it over to her?"

"Great idea," I said with a smile.

Then we enjoyed the sun for a while until the heat chased us into the ocean, where we dodged surfers and little kids. The water was warm, and we ended up body surfing in the waves, something I hadn't done since I was a kid. I'd forgotten how much fun it was.

Chapter Seven

When we got back to Holly's place, it was getting close to suppertime. I'd managed to dredge from my memory Holly's favorite takeout Chinese meal in college. We picked it up, along with some food for Grayson and me. Then, with a little trepidation, we walked in.

Holly looked pale, but composed. She gave me a hug, holding me tightly when she saw the food. "Y'all are the best."

"Everything going okay?" I asked. I made a face. "Never mind. I know nothing is actually going okay."

"I guess it's going as well as could be expected. I poured myself a glass of wine and called my parents." She closed her eyes for a moment. "Yeah, it was pretty bad. It's the kind of news that really should be delivered in person, but I couldn't put off telling them in order to catch a flight up there."

"I'm so sorry," I breathed. "I know that must have been awful."

Holly took a deep breath. "Yeah. Well, at least that's over now." She paused. "I've been thinking about other people I should call. I'm just not sure who the police have talked to and who they haven't. I was also working a little on Frank's obituary. When that runs in the *Post and Courier*, that will definitely help spread the news."

Grayson said, "Holly and I could make some calls for you, if you'd like. If you can pull together a list of names and phone numbers."

She gave him a smile. "Thanks. But the more I thought about it, the more I figured people were going to find out pretty quickly. Charleston, in a lot of ways, functions like a small town. The only call I thought I might make was to Frank's dental practice. But when Warner was telling us about Frank's business partner, it made me think that the police might have run by there this afternoon to notify them. And, maybe, to ask some questions."

I nodded. "That makes sense. It sounded like things were probably pretty tense between the two of them. I can understand Carl wanting to leave Charleston, but he was asking a lot to pressure Frank to sell."

Holly said, "That's what I thought, too. It's not as if Frank was going to stop practicing dentistry. He wasn't retirement age or anything. Carl was basically putting him in the position of asking him to find another practice. And Frank didn't want to do that. I'm not saying Carl had anything to do with this, but what if he got really frustrated with Frank and lashed out at him? It could have been totally unpremeditated. Maybe he was just letting off some steam and shoved at the bookcase without even thinking about the consequences."

Holly's doorbell rang, startling us all. Holly walked over to the door. She opened it to a pretty, well-groomed woman with long, honey-colored hair and a determined expression on her face.

"June," said Holly, looking surprised.

June gave Holly a tense smile. "Hey, Holly. Sorry to barge in like this." She glanced behind Holly and spotted Grayson and me. "Oh, were you entertaining?" Her expression suggested that she thought it was in poor taste, considering what had happened.

Holly said, "June, this is Ann and Grayson. Ann was my roommate in college. You might have heard me talk about her." She hesitated. "June was married to Frank."

June nodded. "Nice to meet you." She turned back to Holly. "Sorry to bug you, but I needed to find out more about what happened. The cops came by to talk to me, and I just had no idea what was going on. They didn't want to fill me in, either. It was maddening. I don't know where they got off, thinking they could ask me questions and not answer any of mine."

"They told you what happened to Frank, though?" asked Holly in a quiet voice.

"Yes." June paused. "I'm sorry, Holly. That news must have been awful for you to hear."

Holly swallowed hard. "It's not been a great day. But I'm not sure I know much more than you do. The police were definitely keeping information to themselves."

June waved a hand around. I couldn't help but notice the huge engagement ring on her finger. "The cops were the worst! I mean, they work for *us*. We're taxpayers, right? They weren't helpful in the slightest."

The way June was talking made her sound a little like an airhead. But I couldn't help but wonder if that was an act. Those determined eyes were bright with intelligence and energy. And Frank hadn't seemed like the kind of guy who would be interested in an airhead.

June continued, "They wanted to know where I was when it happened. I was like, 'how do I know? I don't know when Frank died.' So they told me and I explained I was getting everything boxed up at my place. Getting ready to move. Moving is very hard work, and the cops didn't act like it was at all. They didn't think that was an alibi."

"Nobody was there with you, helping you pack?" asked Holly.

June snorted. "Do you think it's easy to get somebody to help you pack stuff up? Plus, it was in the morning on a workday. If I'd known I was going to need an alibi, I'd have ordered pizza and told everyone it was a party. How was I supposed to know there was a crime committed? It seems like the system is totally prejudiced against innocent people." She waved her diamond-encrusted hand again.

Holly took the bait. "That's a beautiful ring," she said lightly. "Is Paul the lucky guy?"

June gave a somewhat simpering smile. "It's pretty, isn't it? And you're right—it is Paul."

Holly looked stunned, and it took her a moment to respond. When she did, she looked at Grayson and me. "Paul is the mayor of Charleston," she said. "And an old family friend."

June put her left hand over her mouth, the rock of a diamond twinkling at us. "I'm sorry, Holly. It's probably impolite to talk about a new fiancé to one's ex-sister-in-law."

Holly was looking exhausted, but she smiled at June. "Not at all. I hope you'll be really happy with him. He's a great guy."

June's eyes lit up. "You *must* come to the engagement party. I insist. Did Paul send you an invitation?"

Holly pressed her lips together and shook her head.

"That was just Paul trying to be sensitive, I bet. But he's such great friends with your family that it won't feel right if you're not there. We'll have plenty of food and plenty of alcohol. It's tomorrow night. Bring Grayson and Ann! It's the perfect place for visitors to see . . . it's on a yacht in Charleston Harbor. The weather is supposed to be perfect, so there'll be a spectacular sunset. Plus, great views: the waterways. Say you'll be there."

Holly gave us both a quick, apologetic look, and then agreed. Holly looked even more exhausted now than she had before June came in. It was as if June had drained her of the little energy she had left.

June continued, making a face. "I feel just so awful that I haven't been in touch with Frank for a while. It made me sad to call him, though . . . I missed him. I know that seems weird to say, doesn't it?" The question was directed at Holly.

Holly said in a tight voice, "Maybe a little, since I believe you were the one who instigated the divorce."

June gave a tight smile. "That's true. But still, whenever I spoke with Frank, I had this wave of regret wash over me. We had a lot of shared history together, you know. Lots of good times. It gave me a feeling of nostalgia." She quickly added, "But I do know I'm doing the right thing by marrying Paul. Frank and I were better as friends. It makes me *furious* that someone did this. Somebody took my friend away from me. I'd like to hunt them down myself."

Holly said, "I didn't realize you and Frank were still so friendly."

Holly's tone made me wonder if she disputed June's claim. She'd told Grayson and me earlier than she hadn't thought their divorce had been a friendly one.

June said, "Oh, Frank and I just didn't see eye-to-eye on some things. Frank was always so . . . content."

June said this as if it were an undesirable trait. Something Frank had needed to work on and improve at—becoming less content.

"He was just never one to strive for more," said June with a shrug of her thin shoulders. "His passion was in his hobby. The only problem was that I didn't connect with his hobbies. But I respected him for being so smart."

Holly said, sounding sad, "I never really connected with Frank's hobby, either. I'm wishing now that I'd listened closer when he was talking about it. Do you know more about the relic hunting than I do?"

June made a face. "Probably not. But I know he was taking more and more time away from his dental practice to fit in relic hunting. That was one of the things we didn't see eye-to-eye on. I didn't understand why he'd be spending so much time doing something that wasn't bringing in money."

Grayson cleared his throat. "We saw one of Frank's colleagues today. He mentioned Frank had definitely had at least one successful dig."

June's eyes widened. "Oh, you're talking about the Spanish coins. Right! Yes, that one was pretty amazing. But Frank didn't want to sell them! That's what would drive me crazy. There are all kinds of collectors online who'd love to buy that kind of stuff off of him. Plus, museums always expressed an interest.

But Frank usually wanted to hold on to the things he dug up. He liked going around and talking about the relics to different groups and looking at them in shadow boxes. I couldn't understand it."

Holly said, "Do you have any idea who might have been upset with Frank? Maybe that guy, Warner?"

June frowned. "Warner? Was that one of those men he'd meet up with from time to time? I don't know much about him. I tried to stay out of the way when Frank had those guys over."

"But he came to your house sometimes?" pressed Holly.

"Sure. But I think you're on the wrong track, Holly. That guy was a total wimp. I can't see him murdering anybody, much less somebody as fit as Frank was."

I exchanged a glance with Grayson. June clearly didn't know that it wasn't the kind of murder that would have pitted Frank against anybody. All it took was a shove of a heavy bookcase, and it was all over. The police clearly weren't releasing that information. The only reason we'd known is because we'd spoken with Meredith, the librarian.

June continued, "I'm thinking you should look more at that awful woman Frank had started dating. Mindy? Cindy?"

Holly corrected her. "Lindy. Lindy Baker." Holly's eyes opened wide, and she covered her mouth with her hands. "Oh no. I totally forgot to call Lindy."

I said quietly, "I'm sure the police have notified her by now."

Holly briefly closed her eyes. "Yes. But they wouldn't have known how close she was to Frank. They'd have just notified her like any other employee. Oh, I can't believe I forgot to call her."

June raised her eyebrows. "Hey, it's not like you weren't under any stress today. I wouldn't worry about it. It's easy to forget stuff when you're stressed out. Did you even know Lindy?"

Holly nodded. "Yeah, I'd met her a few times. Actually, I really like her. I thought she and Frank made a good couple."

June's expression was disdainful. "Lindy would never have made Frank happy. I mean, I didn't actually know her, but I spoke to her on the phone every now and then when I'd call Frank's office. And everybody knows you're not supposed to date somebody you work with."

I asked, "Lindy works at the dental practice?"

Holly nodded. "She's the receptionist and bookkeeper there."

June was clearly tired of talking about Frank. She gave us all a smile. "Well, I guess I better be taking myself home. I just wanted to come by and tell you how sorry I was, Holly."

I thought that hadn't been the reason she'd dropped by at all. She'd been there to try to find out more information. I wondered if Frank's death would be a source of gossip on that yacht the following night.

Holly saw June out and leaned briefly against the door as June's high heels clicked against the walkway heading out to her car. "That was exhausting."

Chapter Eight

I stood up and said, "Let me get you something to eat. Or something to drink."

Holly shook her head. "I'm fine, thanks. It's just been a really stressful day. Plus, I've never enjoyed spending time with June. She's always so intense and pushy. And she clearly was over here just to see what she could find out."

"Did she and Frank have a friendly breakup?" asked Grayson curiously.

Holly snorted. "Not at all. June said some really unfair things about Frank. You heard her—she didn't like the fact that Frank wasn't ambitious or a social climber. Social climbing is what June is all about. And money. June was never really satisfied with Frank's income or his reluctance to spend it. And now I'm wondering if this relationship with the mayor started before Frank and June's marriage was even over, even if Frank didn't think that was so. To make it even worse, Frank and Paul were best friends."

My eyes opened wide. "Frank was best friends with the mayor? The guy June is marrying?"

"That's right," said Holly. "We grew up together. Frank and Paul hung out every day. Frank couldn't believe that the two of them would betray him like that." Holly shook her head. "I thought Lindy Baker, the receptionist, was going to be a much better match for Frank than June was. June always acted like she looked down on Frank and the different things he liked to do. Like I mentioned, she's a total social climber. All she wanted to do was go out and meet up with people and network. Buy beautiful clothes and purses. But Frank's idea of fun was to do relic hunting in his off hours."

Grayson said, "Sounds like their lifestyles and goals really weren't in sync."

"Exactly," said Holly. "I mean, June was fine. We got along okay whenever we were thrown together. But I always thought she was hard on Frank, you know? The way she'd push and prod him made it sound like she thought he was just totally inadequate. She complained about the amount of time he spent apart from her." She shrugged. "I mean, I had some sympathy for her there. Frank would go to the office to see his patients, then he'd be off doing his relic hunting after work or on the weekends. June really didn't get to spend much time with him."

I said slowly, "And June would have no reason to do something like this, right?"

"I can't see her hurting Frank. And why would she? It's not as if he didn't consent to a divorce. And they don't have children, so there was no dispute regarding custody. Plus, I don't think she and Frank cared enough about each other to be that upset that things were over between them. But I'm sure the police are probably going to be asking her a lot of questions. I'm sure she's going to hate that. Image is everything."

I said, "Is that why she's engaged to Paul, do you think?"

Holly grimaced. "That's such a mess. If I didn't know June better, I'd think she'd hooked up with Paul just to get back at Frank. But like I said, I don't think either Frank nor June was really all that upset about the end of their marriage. But sure—the fact that Paul is mayor, wealthy, and has a lot of connections would be very attractive to June." She paused. "While we're discussing Paul, I just wanted to let you both know that I just don't feel up to going to an engagement party tomorrow night."

"Of course you don't," I said.

Grayson quickly added, "We'll just make excuses and not go."

Holly shook her head. "Unfortunately, it's probably not that easy. I'm sure June, Type-A person who she is, is probably already on the phone making arrangements for an extra table. If it's not too much to ask, it would be awesome if you could make an appearance on my behalf. I know that's probably a real imposition, but you'd really be doing me a favor. I feel rotten even asking you. But June is the kind of person to hold a grudge."

I frowned. "Hold a grudge? Your brother just died. Plus, she's your brother's *ex-wife*. She was being pretty insensitive to have invited you at all."

"I know. But that's the way she is. If the two of you say I suddenly had a migraine, she won't be as upset."

Grayson said, "Of course we'll go. Right, Ann?"

Ordinarily, this would be the last thing I'd want to do. But I realized this would give me the opportunity to speak with Paul, the mayor. Part of me thought maybe I could help find a little information that I could pass on to the lieutenant. If someone was arrested for the crime, maybe it would help Holly move forward.

"Of course we will," I agreed.

Holly relaxed a little, looking relieved. "Thanks so much, guys."

That night, though, I had trouble falling asleep. My mind kept thinking about Frank and the different people who might be suspects. Fitz's eyes glowed in the dark. The last time I checked my watch was two a.m., after which I fell into a restless sleep.

The next morning, Grayson headed into town for his appointment with the attorney. That suited me fine because I rolled over and went back to sleep after being awake half the night. I didn't hear any sounds from downstairs yet, so I hoped Holly was doing the same thing.

An hour later, I finally got up, showered, dressed, and headed downstairs. Holly was in the kitchen and was wrapping up a phone call.

"Got it. All right—tomorrow at two. Thanks." Holly hung up with a sigh. "The funeral home. I'm meeting with them tomorrow. Of course, I'm not sure when Frank will be released to the funeral home. I know there'll likely be an autopsy." She rubbed the side of her face with her hand.

"Is there anything I can help you with?" I asked. "Any phone calls or anything? Grayson is meeting with the attorney right now."

"I figured. No, you're all good. I've just got a couple more phone calls to make. I've taken some days off from work. Mom and Dad were completely devastated, as I thought they might be, and I'm glad I can step in to help plan the funeral service."

"Have you heard anything more from the police?" I asked.

Holly shook her head. "Not yet. I guess that means they don't have any additional information. And haven't made an arrest."

"I know it would probably be easier for you, in some ways, if there *was* an arrest. I hope that happens soon."

Holly said, "That reminds me. I had something I wanted to ask you. You're sure you're good about you and Grayson going to the engagement party tonight?"

"Sure, that's no problem at all. You're still wanting us to go, right?"

Holly nodded. "Yes, that would be great. It'll be like I have a representative there in my place, which will help smooth things over with June." She leaned in, as if we might be overheard, despite being the only creatures in the house besides Murphy and Fitz. "I remember your telling me that you'd helped with murder investigations in Whitby before."

"Very, very unofficially. It's one of those things where I'm in the position to speak with people casually and sometimes overhear information. Then I can pass what I hear over to the police."

Holly said, "That's actually very useful for the cops. After all, people have their guards up around police officers. But they wouldn't around their friendly, neighborhood librarian." She paused. "I don't want to ask you to do anything you're uncomfortable doing."

"You'd like me to poke around a little tonight, maybe?" I asked. Of course, I'd already been thinking along those lines myself. Especially when it came to the mayor.

Holly smiled at me. "I'd love it if you would. I know the police won't be present at a private function like an engagement party, and I bet it will be a good time to talk to Paul. And June again, I suppose. Who knows—maybe there will be other people there who might know something, too."

I thought that the last bit might be a stretch, but I nodded my head. "I'll be very discreet."

"I doubt you even have to be. I know that crowd—they're very outgoing. What's more, they're going to be interested in hearing what *you* know about what happened to Frank." Holly's voice broke when she said her brother's name, and she took a couple of deep breaths to collect herself.

"You're probably right. I'll play everything very low-key and see what I can find out. Then I can share whatever information I have with the lieutenant."

Holly nodded absently, now intent again on the legal pad where she'd scribbled early funeral service plans. "Sounds good."

"What plans are you thinking about for the service?" I asked.

"Oh, I was thinking about something really simple. Probably a celebration of life service. If we do that, we can have a private family burial later on, whenever the police release Frank's body." She shook her head. "I still can't believe it. But I'm trying. There's too much to do to be in any kind of denial."

"When are your parents coming in?"

Holly said, "Tomorrow. I think they're *also* having a tough time believing it, and they think coming to Charleston will help them wrap their heads around it all. I'm not sure it will, but I hope it helps. They sounded completely devastated."

I heard a car pulling up to the house. "Grayson must be back," I said.

Holly stood. "I should take a shower and get ready to take on my day." She headed upstairs, with Murphy following excitedly behind her. Fitz passed Murphy on the stairs, and Murphy gave him a big, sloppy kiss, which Fitz took with equanimity. When Fitz finally made it downstairs, though, he immediately started bathing himself, as if to remove all the Murphy cooties.

Grayson came in, carrying a folder and wearing a bemused expression on his face.

"Everything okay?" I asked. "How did it go with the attorney's office?"

Grayson said slowly, "It was fine. He was a nice guy. But the bequest was a lot larger than I thought."

"That's nice, though, isn't it?" I asked. Grayson and I were in the same boat with our income levels. Being a librarian and a newspaper editor in a small town didn't bring in a lot of money.

"Yeah. But I was just kind of stunned. My uncle always lived a very simple life. Apparently, according to his lawyer, he'd always socked away any extra money he had in the stock market. And with compounding and everything . . . "

I said ruefully, "You're going to lose me quickly if you start getting into math."

Grayson said with a slow smile, "The bottom line is that I suddenly have a good deal of money."

"A good deal?" I asked.

"Yes. Like I could buy a large house," said Grayson.

"A large house in Whitby?"

Grayson said, "I think I could even buy a large house in Charleston."

I felt my jaw drop a little. Grayson nodded. "It's really crazy. Knowing my uncle, I figured I'd end up with his car and maybe a few thousand dollars or something. I just stared at the lawyer when he was telling me about the will."

"That's unreal," I said.

"I know. Of course, it has to make its way through probate and everything. But eventually, that money is going to land in my bank account." He shook his head. "I'm just stunned."

"What about his house and car and things? Are you going to need to spend a lot of time down here clearing things out?"

Grayson said, "He did actually leave his house and car to my parents. I'm glad, because this would make me feel really guilty otherwise. I'll plan a trip back down here later to help them clear it out. But there shouldn't be much stuff. Like I said, my uncle led a pretty bare-bones existence."

He sat down at the kitchen table with me and I poured a cup of coffee and put it in front of him. Grayson really looked like he needed something to snap him out of the disbelief he was feeling. "What do you think you'll do with it?" I asked, "Do you *want* a big house?"

"No. I don't really want anything much. I never liked the idea of collecting a ton of stuff. Besides, I'm comfortable with the way I'm living. I've got all the space I need. And I love Whitby. We're both living in a vacation destination, you know."

I nodded. Whitby, with its lake and mountains, was a popular tourist destination for western North Carolina. Besides the outdoor activities, there were a lot of cute places to shop, too.

Grayson took a sip of his coffee. "It will be nice not to have to worry so much about whether or not the newspaper loses subscribers. Or whether our ad revenue drops."

"Security is good."

"It sure is," said Grayson. "But aside from socking money away for a rainy day, I think what I'm most interested in is having experiences."

"Travel?" I asked.

"Right. I've always wanted to do a sort of great American tour. See Yellowstone and the Grand Canyon and all of that. Take some time to take it all in." He paused. "Of course, it's more fun when you do that stuff with somebody else." He smiled at me.

"Sounds great. But you'll have to give me plenty of advance notice if you want me to take time off work. Wilson will probably need high blood pressure medicine. I have a tough time breaking away from the library. You know how hard it was to even slip away to Charleston, and it's not even all that far away."

"Don't worry, I'll give you plenty of upfront warning. Besides, it'll take me forever to plan out a travel itinerary and stuff like that." Grayson shook his head in wonder. "It's just not something I thought I'd ever really do. At least not for a long time." He thought some more. "I'd also like to give money to some of the local charities in Whitby. It's going to take a while to figure all this out."

"Maybe you should see a financial planner," I noted. "A fiduciary, so they're totally unbiased. They can advise you and maybe help you invest, too. That way, your money will continue growing."

"Spoken like a true librarian," said Grayson with a smile. "And you're absolutely right." He paused and glanced upstairs. "How is Holly doing today?"

"She seems okay. She's planning Frank's service. Her parents are coming in tomorrow, she thinks."

Grayson asked, "Will we be able to go to the service while we're here? Or will it be later?" He lowered his voice. "Won't the police have to release Frank's body?"

"Holly is planning to do a celebration of life service and a private burial later. So it sounds like it might be possible we'll be able to make the funeral."

"Good," Grayson said. "I'd like to go to it."

"In the meantime, what do you want to do with the rest of your day?" I asked. "Are you feeling like a quiet day? Maybe another day on the beach? Or would you like to go sightsee and eat out and that kind of thing? Or, since you're such a money-bag now, would you want to go shopping?"

Grayson snorted. "I'm definitely *not* a moneybag, at least not yet. Maybe we should take it easy today. Let's drive to one of the beaches."

This time, we were a lot more organized. We put together a beach bag and a cooler and headed out to Sullivan's Island this time. We lucked out with public parking and had just a short walk over to the beach.

There was a great breeze coming off the ocean, which made being out there a lot more comfortable. Plus, Grayson had brought more gear this time. He had a tent, for one, that would provide us with some shade while we were out there.

"Want some help with that?" I asked, squinting up at him from my beach towel as he struggled with the tent in the breeze.

"Nope!" he said cheerfully. "I've got it."

But, minutes later, sand covering both himself and the tent, it was clear that he hadn't. I gave him a hand, and he gave me a rueful grin in return. Soon, we had the tent up. Grayson had also brought a mini speaker with him and started playing some music.

"I have to say I'm really impressed with the way you got this all planned," I said.

"Well, I'd meant to bring this stuff out yesterday, but I guess I got kind of rattled with Frank's death."

We let the music and the breeze carry away some of the stress we'd been feeling. Then, after a while, we swam in the ocean, floating on a raft Grayson blew up. Fortunately, there were no surfers here—a good thing, since I'm sure we'd have created quite a hazard as we drifted around aimlessly on the raft, talking just as aimlessly.

We ended up spending the day out there. The tent made it easy to escape from the sun, and there was plenty of food and water for us. It was a beautiful day and reminded me I was actually on vacation.

Around four, I said reluctantly, "We should probably head back and get ready for the engagement party." I had the feeling Grayson didn't mind going to the party at all. He was often a lot more outgoing and extroverted than I was. I was definitely going to the party with more of a dutiful mindset, wanting to help Holly out. Although I did want to ask Paul, Frank's best friend, a few questions.

"Right," said Grayson, stretching. "That should be pretty interesting. I've never been on a yacht before. We'll be mixing it up with some pretty fancy people, I bet. And the view sounds like it's going to be gorgeous."

I frowned. "It suddenly occurs to me that I'm not sure what I'm supposed to wear to this thing."

"Oh, it's the beach. I'm sure we'll be fine. Did you bring anything that's business casual?"

I had to think through my carefully packed bag. "I brought a black top, but it's pretty basic. And a black skirt. I hope that's going to work. How about you?"

"I have the outfit that I wore to the attorney's office—khakis and a button-down. We can ask Holly to make sure they'll work."

Chapter Nine

When we got to Holly's house, she wasn't there. She'd given us a key earlier and had left a note on the counter saying that she was out running errands.

"I'm going to text her about the dress code," I said.

Grayson grinned at me. "You're making it sound like you're back in high school and trying to make sure your shorts aren't too short."

"True, ha. I'll ask her what the attire is supposed to be for the party."

Holly got back to me right away. "I'm sure business casual will be fine."

I told her what I'd brought and asked if it would work. There was a longer pause between texts this time. "Take a sundress from my closet," Holly texted.

I showed Grayson my phone, and he chuckled. "I guess she wasn't as sure about your outfit."

"At least she and I are about the same size."

A couple of hours later, we were cleaned up and ready to go. Holly returned from her errands and helped me pick out the perfect dress from her closet. It was a long floral A-line dress with a halter top. The flower print was in vibrant shades of pink. Luckily, *I* wasn't in a vibrant shade of pink because I'd carefully applied sunscreen throughout our beach day. I'd gotten a little too much on one of my knees (I wasn't sure how I missed spots like that), but the dress covered it up.

"I wonder how big this yacht is," said Grayson.

"Not sure. Is there such a thing as a *small* yacht? I thought most yachts were pretty big." I made a quick search on my phone. "It looks like a fifty-two-foot yacht holds twelve people."

Grayson said, "The way June was talking, it sounded like there were going to be a lot more people than just twelve. Otherwise, we wouldn't have gotten an invite."

We found out minutes later, after reaching the dock, that the yacht was indeed big. This was no fifty-two-foot yacht.

Grayson gave a low whistle. "That's got to be at least 100 feet. And it has two decks."

There were already a lot of people there. Upwards of fifty, for sure.

"This can't be a private yacht, can it?" asked Grayson.

"It's got to be a chartered yacht." I pulled out my phone again and looked up the name of the boat, *Carpe Diem*. "Yes, it's chartered."

We joined the line for boarding, and I saw, to my relief, that Grayson and I fit in just fine with what we were wearing. But it was probably a good thing I hadn't shown up in a black top and black skirt. The women were all wearing colorful dresses. Some men were in seersucker suits, but many of them were in khakis and polos like Grayson.

Inside there was a full bar, caterers manning long buffet tables, and tables covered with white tablecloths. Music played in the background and a man holding a drink in one hand and a cordless microphone in the other was giving an emotional speech about his friendship with Paul Hammond.

I could tell right away who Paul was. The mayor of Charleston looked uncomfortable at the man's speech. For someone who spent a lot of time in the limelight, he seemed very unhappy being in it tonight. He had a tight smile pasted on his face, which didn't quite reach his eyes. I could see lines of stress around his mouth and eyes, and he looked tired, as if he hadn't been sleeping.

Overall, I could see why June had been attracted to him. He had an attractive, sort of fraternity boy look about him. He was certainly young to be a mayor. He wore preppy clothes—a pink checkered button-down shirt and a navy sport coat—with a careless air, although I suspected his appearance was carefully engineered. He had thick, dark hair. When he finally smiled, after the man had stopped speaking, I saw a flash of a dimple and white teeth.

No one else seemed to be walking up to give a toast, and I saw relief cross Paul's features. His gaze flickered across the room, resting on Grayson and me. That could be because we were standing there awkwardly, not knowing anyone, and not sure if we wanted to get drinks or get food. Paul walked over to us.

I glanced around to see if I could spot June. She was far across the room, surrounded by a large group of people and laughing.

"I'm starting to feel like a party crasher," murmured Grayson. "I wonder if we're about to be thrown out."

"June can vouch for us," I said. I tried to sound confident, although I was feeling nervous. June gave a loud peal of laughter that reverberated throughout the ship.

"I think June might be plastered," said Grayson ruefully.

I didn't have the chance to respond because Paul had quickly stepped up to us, extending a hand. "Paul Hammond," he said quickly. "I don't think I've had the pleasure of meeting you."

I'd seen Grayson in action as a reporter before. He was always smooth, friendly, and seemed genuinely interested in the person he was talking to. It was Reporter Grayson now. He gave Paul a big smile and held his hand out. "Grayson Phillips. This is my friend, Ann Beckett."

Paul's smile became more genuine. "Ah, Holly's friends." His face suddenly fell. "How is Holly? I'm not surprised she didn't feel she could make it tonight."

I could tell he really wanted to know the answer, instead of asking just to be polite.

I said, "She's hanging in there. Her parents are coming into town tomorrow. She said to tell you congratulations, and that she was sorry she couldn't make it. She had a migraine."

Paul nodded absently. "I feel like I've fallen down on the job by not going over to see Holly yesterday. Frank and I grew up like brothers. We hung out all the time—even *fought* like brothers. I loved that guy."

There was a wild cheer as the music played a disco tune, and Paul grimaced. "Let's head onto the deck for a moment so we can talk."

He ushered us to a quiet spot on the deck. The boat had sailed away from the slip and was heading out into the open water. I could already see that there was indeed going to be a beautiful sunset. It was almost as if Paul and June had expressly ordered it for the night.

Paul looked relieved to have escaped the hoopla and general noise of the party. "That's better," he said. "I'm just not in the mood for any of this tonight. Frank's death hit me badly. I wanted to push back the engagement party, but June wouldn't hear of it." He looked rather irritated by this.

"I know Frank's death came as an awful shock," I said.

Paul let out a big sigh. "It did. I thought the police had somehow gotten things confused. I couldn't believe something had happened to Frank. I'd just seen him the day-before-yesterday—we grabbed lunch together. I was distracted because of some things going on at the office. I wish I'd known that was going to be the last time we saw each other, although we had a brief phone call later." He cast a brooding look over the water for a minute. Then he added, "Has Holly heard much from the police? Do they have any leads?"

I shook my head. "As far as I'm aware, she's only spoken with the police once, when they notified her about Frank's death."

Grayson asked, "The police spoke with you?"

If possible, Paul looked even more exhausted than he already did. "That's right. I believe they were trying to establish a timeline for Frank's death. Who he'd spoken to last, where he was, what he was working on." He paused. "I'd spoken with Frank briefly yesterday morning."

"Do you think your conversation might help the police figure out who did this?" asked Grayson.

Paul shook his head. "Doubtful. There wasn't much of anything to it. The officer had a couple of questions about the engagement party. I was very busy at the office and was in and out of meetings."

"So you were able to provide the police with an alibi, then," I guessed.

"Unfortunately, some of the meetings were around town, so I'm not sure I did. That's why I was interested in finding out what the police had found out, or if any arrest had been made. I'm not very comfortable being a suspect in a murder case. And I already felt bad enough because I blew Frank off when he called me."

"I'm sure it wasn't that bad," said Grayson.

Paul shrugged. "It feels that way to me. As I've gotten older, sometimes I feel more distracted. I guess it's just modern life. There's always a phone notification going off or an email coming in. Everything at work is presented to me as if it were an emergency that needs to be immediately acted on."

"That sounds frustrating," said Grayson, sounding sympathetic.

"It is. Worse, because the distraction I mentioned keeps me from being fully present with people I care about. Or even people I *don't* care about. I'm just nodding my head and saying, 'Um-hmm' and not giving my full attention to what the person is saying. That's what happened during that last phone call. Frank was asking me about the party, and I was listening with half an ear while I was scrolling through my list of upcoming meetings."

I said, "It sounds like you simply have your hands full. You've got a busy job with a lot of different moving parts. Maybe you've tried multitasking to just get everything done each day. I don't think Frank would want you beating yourself up over this."

Paul gave me an appreciative look. "You're right. Thanks. He wasn't like that at all. Did you spend much time with Frank?"

"Not too much. He would come for family weekends sometimes when Holly and I were in college. He was pretty quiet then."

Paul chuckled. "You must have caught Frank when he was feeling awkward. Being at his sister's college during a family weekend sounds exactly like the kind of thing that would make him uncomfortable. Usually, Frank was full of energy, running his mouth. But he was also a real academic." He made a wry face. "A much better student than I was. The only reason I got an occasional B was because Frank would ask if he and I could study together at the library."

"Was he always interested in history?" I asked. "I understand he was a relic hunter."

I spotted a brief, unrecognizable emotion pass quickly across Paul's handsome features before he smiled and said, "He was interested in history. In fact, he was a double major in college. He was always something of an overachiever. Frank was getting a biology major to help him with his dentistry career path, but he was taking history for fun. I remember thinking that he had lost his mind."

Grayson laughed. "Was he spending a lot of time studying?"

"He sure was. I was always trying to get him to come to a big party at my fraternity house or something. There were always lots of cute girls there. But he'd say he had to study or write a paper or something. There were *tons* of papers for his history major. I mean, I had to satisfy my liberal arts history requirement, so I took a class on American history. But Frank was taking classes on Middle Eastern politics and women and gender studies. He was always in the library surrounded by huge tomes and looking up facts on government internet sites." Paul's mouth pulled into a small smile, remembering.

He looked at both of us. "I need to run by and see Holly. I totally understand why she's not here tonight, like I mentioned. But I need to go pay my respects. I picked up the phone to reach out to Holly earlier, but then I stopped." He gave a deep sigh. "I'm one of those people who thinks you shouldn't burden somebody with your own grief. Especially when they have even more reason to grieve than you do. I figured I should wait and see Holly when I can speak to her without choking up. I didn't want to put her in the position of having to comfort *me* when she has so much more to grieve."

There were more squeals of laughter and raucous voices from inside as a different song came on. Paul shook his head. "My head is just not in the right place to handle this party tonight. I should have just rescheduled, even if it meant losing the deposits and pushing back the wedding. I don't feel right celebrating right now."

Grayson, who always had the mind of a reporter even when he was away from his beat, asked, "I'm sorry if this is an impertinent question. But there's one thing I was wondering."

Paul gave him a crooked smile in return. "You're wondering if Frank's and my relationship was impacted by my relationship with June?" He gave a short laugh. "Don't worry—that's been something on everybody's mind. Believe it or not, Frank didn't harbor any bad feelings about June and me." He looked down at his hands, which were clasped in front of him. "I'd admired June for a long time. I guess she must have realized it. I never acted on it until they'd both started divorce proceedings. Frank took our relationship in stride. Of course, the police seemed to have their own opinions on whether that was actually the case. Naturally, they thought I had a pretty big motive to get rid of Frank."

I frowned. "Really? Why? After all, it sounds like Frank granted the divorce and didn't seem too affected by the end of his marriage."

Paul shrugged again. "I guess the cops figured I might still be jealous of Frank somehow and wanted to eliminate my competition once and for all."

I figured Paul's fiancée might also be a suspect. Grayson and I glanced at each other.

Paul probably guessed what was going through our minds. Perhaps to divert attention away from June and himself, he said, "I gave the police a lead on someone who could be a *real* suspect. Frank's business partner had plenty of cause to want him gone."

"The dentist?" Grayson's voice suggested that he didn't, as a rule, find dentists particularly dangerous.

We'd already been told about Carl's desire to sell the dental practice and move closer to his aging mother. But I was curious to see what Paul had to say.

Paul continued, "Frank told me that Carl had a great offer from somebody to take over the practice, and he wanted to sell it, lock, stock, and barrel. Frank hadn't been interested in selling at all."

"Did Frank say why he didn't want to leave?" asked Grayson.

Paul shrugged. "Why would he? He was perfectly happy there. The practice has its own parking lot, and it's centrally located. He had plenty of patients. There's a great deli next door where he could grab a healthy lunch . . . he and I often ate there. He had no reason to move. I'm wondering if his partner might have done him in. He'd have realized that Frank could be stubborn."

Grayson asked, "What was Frank like? Aside from being a little stubborn, I mean? I know you said he was a good student and very academic."

I was wondering much the same thing and admired Grayson's casual manner of asking questions. I hadn't really known Frank, and I didn't want to ask Holly about him and risk making her more upset than she already was. Of course, Paul had also been very close to Frank. I wondered if thinking about his friend was going to put him back in his funk.

But it seemed to have the opposite effect. Paul appeared to enjoy the opportunity to talk about Frank. "Well, he sure wasn't motivated by money. That wasn't something that had any appeal for Frank. Besides, his family had plenty of money, and he had money of his own."

Grayson nodded. "So if Carl had tried to tempt him with money?"

Paul snorted. "If his partner had tried to dangle a big payout in front of him to convince him to sell the practice, it wouldn't have had any effect on Frank. He was a fastidious guy in a lot of ways—even in college. His dorm room was obsessively tidy. Well, tidy on Frank's side, anyway. His roommate's side looked like a bomb had gone off. But even though the mess probably drove Frank crazy, he never said a word. He wasn't an argumentative type of guy. I wasn't surprised to hear that June and Frank had separated completely amicably."

"It seems like he was a pretty driven guy," said Grayson. "He had a successful dental practice, from what I understand, and was equally successful with his hobby."

Paul nodded. "That's right. He was one of those 'slow and steady wins the race' people. He was hugely routine-driven. I think that's one reason he could accomplish so much. He always got up at 4:30 or 5:00 in the morning and jumped in right away." Paul shook his head. "I admired that about him."

I said, "Well, you're not exactly a slouch, yourself. You've also got to be a driven person to be as young as you are and to be mayor of Charleston."

Paul stiffed a little. "I'm not sure about that. I just did what was expected of me. And I'm usually a pretty outgoing guy, although you can't tell that tonight. I just exploited my connections."

It surprised me to hear Paul talk like this about his role in local government. It sounded almost as if he disliked what he was doing or felt almost embarrassed about it. Most politicians, when asked, would go on and on about how it was a privilege to serve the community. Paul seemed as if he couldn't be less interested in talking about his job.

Since he appeared to be uncomfortable with the subject, I changed it. "Did you and Holly spend a lot of time together when you were growing up?"

Now a smile tugged at Paul's lips at the memories. "We sure did. Although we didn't want to. Frank and I were always trying to get away from Frank's kid sister. But that was easier said than done. Holly had this gift of knowing exactly where we were in the neighborhood and joining us. Plus, Frank's parents thought we needed to include Holly, so he was always getting lectured to have her hang out with us. Considering how we weren't the nicest to her, it was amazing she wanted to spend so much time with us. She tagged along everywhere. We tried to lose her one time by climbing a tree, and she scrambled right up after us."

"Spunky," said Grayson with a smile.

Paul said, "Yes, but then she fell right back out of it again and broke her arm. We caught a lot of trouble for that, as you can imagine."

The door to the deck opened, and a woman said to the people behind her, "Here he is! Paul, come on! June wants to dance with you."

Paul gave us a wry look. "That's my signal. Thanks for helping me play hooky for a while. It was good meeting you."

Chapter Ten

We watched him go inside. "Should we go too?" Grayson asked.

"Not if we don't want to," I said quickly. "I'm pretty sure the buffet tables are going to be out for a while."

Grayson settled back on the bench with a satisfied sigh. "I was hoping you would say that. I was feeling pretty comfortable out here with the breeze and the view."

The view was beautiful. It was quiet out on the water right now, and the sun was setting. The sky was vibrant, with shades of pink, orange, and purple. They could see the city in the distance.

After a few minutes, I glanced over at Grayson. He was so quiet that I'd suspected he'd nodded off. Then I saw he was just deep in thought.

"Sorry," he said, giving me a small smile. "I guess I have a lot on my mind."

"Of course you do." I paused. "Have you been thinking about your uncle?"

He nodded. "A lot. Thinking about what a surprise it was to get this legacy. And feeling pretty undeserving. I should have reached out more to him."

I said, "Well, it sounds like this is what he *wanted*."

Grayson smiled again. "You're right. I'm going to have to put some thought into what to do with it all."

We chatted quietly for a while outside. Then we enjoyed a huge spread of food. There were lots of fresh shrimp, chicken pot pies, Southern fried chicken, and lots of sides.

June gave us a wave and a thumbs-up when she spotted us at the table. But, still dancing, she didn't come over, which was probably just as well. After eating all the food and following the recent stress, we were both feeling tired. At least we'd had the chance for her to see us and realize we were there.

When we got back to Holly's house, she was in her pjs and a robe. But instead of looking relaxed, she was looking a little shaken. "I should have told Lindy what happened. Frank's girlfriend. I was thinking about Lindy when we were talking to June, but then it totally slipped my mind again."

"It's totally understandable that you wouldn't have immediately reached out," I said. "Frank's death has been a real shock."

Holly rubbed her eyes, looking exhausted. "I know, but still. Maybe part of me thought that Carl, Frank's partner, would have told her. After all, Lindy is his receptionist at the practice. You'd think he'd let her know at least so she could reschedule Frank's appointments."

Grayson said, "That sounds like much more of an oversight on his part than it was on yours."

Holly sighed. "Thanks. I guess Carl has probably been on the phone with whoever he was going to sell the practice to, now that Frank's gone. Anyway, the police called the office and made an appointment to speak with Lindy to speak with her about Frank's murder. They must have been trying to trace Frank's movements, because I'm not sure they knew Lindy and Frank were dating."

I winced a little. That would have been an awful way to find out that something had happened to someone you cared about.

Holly continued, "Lindy called me up sobbing. It was the worst. I'm going to head over to see her tomorrow. Would you go with me, Ann? I don't know Lindy very well and I feel awful about this whole thing."

"Of course I'll go. Grayson and I don't have any set plans for tomorrow." I looked over at Grayson to confirm that, and he nodded at me.

"I'd say the three of us could go, but I thought that might be a little overwhelming for her," said Holly apologetically. She sighed. "I'm sorry. This is the second thing I've asked you to do for me. I promise I'm not usually so bossy."

"I know you're not," I said. "And you're not being bossy now. We want to help any way that we can."

"Thanks." Holly smiled at us. "So how did everything go tonight on the yacht?"

Grayson said, "It was mission accomplished. We saw June, and she acknowledged our presence there."

Holly raised an eyebrow. "That was it? After all that, she didn't come over to greet you or to thank you for being there?"

I said, "She was busy with all the other guests. And with partying. I'm thinking it was good stress relief for her. She didn't seem like the kind of person to let her hair down very often."

Holly snorted. "June isn't. Makes me wish I'd been there after all. I'd have liked to have seen that for comic relief, alone."

"We visited with Paul for a while, though," said Grayson. "He thanked us for being there."

"How was Paul?" asked Holly curiously.

Grayson and I looked at each other. "That's a good question," I said. "He was very quiet and withdrawn. Is that the way he usually is?"

Holly's eyes opened wide. "No, he's never like that. Usually Paul is the typical politician, walking around, glad-handing everybody, and patting folks on the back. He's always campaigning, always looking ahead to the next election, always meeting people and networking. So that's not the way he was tonight?"

We shook our heads. "He wanted to speak with us outside on the deck to get away from the noise and the party."

"And the people," I added. "He didn't seem like he was in any mood to talk to anybody. In fact, he told us he'd wanted to reschedule the engagement party, but June wouldn't hear of it."

Holly knit her brows together. "So, you're saying that Paul Hammond, mayor of Charleston, withdrew from an opportunity to network with tons of well-heeled members of local society to talk outside with y'all?"

I nodded. "For quite a long time."

"Well," she said. "That's pretty remarkable."

Grayson said, "Paul was saying how close he and Frank had been. He was very subdued. I think Frank's death hit him really hard."

"It would have. The two of them were best friends from the start, even though they had very different temperaments and interests." Holly gave us a rueful look. "Did Paul mention the way I tried to tag along with them when we were growing up?"

I grinned at her. "I got the impression they couldn't really escape you."

"They always seemed like they were having more fun than anybody I knew. My mom would try to set me up with playdates with kids my age, but all I wanted to do was try to play with them. I guess I don't mind rejection much. Or maybe I'm just stubborn." Holly gave a yawn. "Okay, well, thanks again for tonight. I'm going to try to turn in early. I didn't sleep well last night. See you both tomorrow."

Chapter Eleven

The next morning looked stormy. There would be bright sun piercing the blue sky, but then a huge, ominous-looking cloud off to the side. It was the kind of day where a thunderstorm could crop up out of nowhere and send rain shooting down. I grabbed my travel umbrella after breakfast when Holly suggested we set out for Lindy's apartment.

"Lindy gave me her address on the phone yesterday," said Holly. "She mentioned she was taking a few days off from work. Lindy seems nice, although I really don't know much about her. Frank thought she was great, I know. I guess a workplace romance is okay in such a small office."

I thought just the opposite, but didn't say so. It seemed to me that in a dental office, with just a few employees, that it could get very awkward very fast if Frank and Lindy ended up being at odds.

Lindy was living in a newer apartment building that was on the outskirts of downtown. She answered the door with swollen, red eyes, and Holly instinctively reached out to give her a hug. Lindy hugged her back, pulling Holly in tight. "I'm so sorry about your brother," Lindy said gruffly.

Lindy was an attractive woman with dark hair and brown eyes. She led us into her tidy, sun-soaked apartment and gestured to a couple of armchairs that looked as if they might be older than Lindy herself.

"I'm just going to grab more tissues," murmured Lindy and hurried away.

Holly and I sat quietly, waiting for her return. It looked as if Lindy's apartment was furnished mainly by what might be family hand-me-downs. She also had numerous books—most in bookcases, but others stacked neatly on top of them.

Lindy returned just as quickly as she'd stepped away, an apologetic expression on her face. "Sorry. It all seems to come over me in waves sometimes," she said, waving a handful of tissues.

"I totally get that," said Holly. She turned to me. "This is my friend, Ann. She's staying with me right now."

Lindy gave me a smile, seemingly incurious about why I might have tagged along with Holly. "Nice to meet you. Would either of you like something to eat or drink?"

We both shook our heads. Holly said, "I wanted to tell you again how sorry I am that I didn't think to call and tell you about Frank. Finding out from the police is terrible."

But Lindy was already waving her hand dismissively. "No apologies needed. You had a terrible shock. Besides, you found out from the police yourself. I know you and Frank were close. I'd just called you up because I wanted to see if you had more information about what happened."

Holly's eyes were regretful. "I'm afraid not. I think knowing more about what happened to Frank would definitely help us process his death. But the police haven't looped me in."

Lindy nodded. "It's okay." She sat quietly for a few moments, looking down at her hands, which were folded in her lap. "I wasn't in the office when it happened. I was taking a slightly longer lunch break in order to run a couple of errands. When I'm out, we let the voice mail grab the calls and then call patients back at lunchtime or the end of the day. It sounded like the police had tried to reach me by phone a couple of times."

Lindy said this in a straightforward manner that made it sound as if it hadn't even really occurred to her that she might be considered a suspect for being out of the office when Frank died. Or that it didn't bother her if she was.

"Did the police ask you who you thought might have a motive to hurt Frank?" asked Holly intently.

Lindy looked mildly surprised at Holly's intensity. That could be why she seemed to be carefully considering her answer. "They did. I was so shocked at the time to hear about Frank's death that I couldn't give the cops anything. But since I've had a little while to think about it, I keep coming back to June."

I thought again about how June had been last night, happily cavorting in the chartered yacht, celebrating her engagement.

"June?" asked Holly. "What makes you think that?"

Lindy quickly said, "I don't have any proof, of course. It's just a feeling."

"June called the office phone yesterday morning. I should have just let the call go to voice mail, but I picked up." Lindy rolled her eyes.

Holly frowned. "Did June call a lot after the divorce?"

"More often than you'd think. I was getting really aggravated, actually, which is probably why I picked up. I felt like giving June a piece of my mind."

Holly asked, "What was June calling him for? Did she say?"

"No, she just wanted him to call her back. And I guess he must not have been returning June's calls on other days, because right off the bat, she accused me of not passing her messages on to him."

I said, "Why didn't June just try to reach Frank on his cell phone?"

Lindy said, "Oh, Frank always turned off his cell phone during the day, so there wasn't any hope of catching him on that. Anyway, she was in a cranky mood."

"You think she might have been upset with Frank and went to find him at the library?" Holly frowned again. "I just can't see why she'd have been upset with him."

Lindy waved her hand around again. "I don't know. It probably wasn't June at all. I just don't like her very much, so I probably am pinning it all on her for that reason. I can't imagine what Frank ever saw in June. It didn't seem like they had anything in common." She shrugged. "Like I said, I just don't like June much. But that doesn't mean she murdered Frank. It's much more likely to have been Carl."

I'd heard a lot about Frank's partner at his dental practice by now. I wondered if Holly and I would find the opportunity to speak with him and hear where he was when Frank died.

Holly just nodded her head. "Because Frank wouldn't sell the practice."

Lindy looked relieved. "Oh, good. You know about that. I worried it might come out of left field. Did Frank tell you?"

"No, but I've heard about it from others. Was Carl really desperate to sell the practice, then?" asked Holly.

"I've never seen him so agitated," said Lindy. "He used to be a lot more laid back about life. But lately, he seemed like he was under a lot of pressure. I think some of it he put on himself.

At first, selling the practice was just something Carl would talk about wistfully."

I said, "So Carl wasn't always so serious about it?"

"That's right. He'd bring up selling the practice to Frank in a friendly manner. Frank would shut him down pretty quickly, and that would be the end of the story."

"But recently, it had gotten worse?" I asked.

Lindy nodded. "I was taking calls, of course. I suddenly started realizing how many were coming in for Carl . . . from his mom. His mother was always sweet and very chatty, so she'd give me an earful about how lonely she was and how much she wished Carl would 'move back home.' I felt sorry for her, honestly. It sounded like she didn't have much of a life; like she really wasn't very connected with people there in the community. I mentioned offhandedly to Carl that maybe it would work better for him to move his mother to Charleston."

"What did he think about that idea?" asked Holly.

"Oh, it was a no-go. Carl said that his mother was dead-set against leaving Wisconsin."

I asked, "Is Carl's father still alive?"

Lindy said, "That's another problem. His father lives with dementia and is in a memory-care unit there. Just another reason Carl's mom wouldn't want to move."

"There are lots of good senior living facilities in Charleston," said Holly.

"I got the impression that Carl was unable or unwilling to stand up to his mom. At any rate, he was feeling a lot of pressure and getting plenty of guilt trips from her. He eventually gave in and said he'd find a way to sell the practice." Lindy flushed.

"That's a conversation I couldn't help but overhear—Carl's office is right behind my desk, and I could hear him when he was on the phone with his mother. But I didn't hear Frank say anything about it. Eventually, I started wondering if Carl had even mentioned it to Frank."

"Until he did," guessed Holly.

"Right. Carl went behind Frank's back to find a buyer for the practice and property. Because it's in such a great location, he found one right away. It was apparently a great offer. Frank told me about it over dinner one night. According to Frank, Carl seemed to think Frank was automatically going to accept it."

Holly frowned again. "Why would Carl think that? It sounds like Frank had already turned him down every time he'd brought the idea up."

Lindy shrugged. "Carl said Frank had been less-focused on his dental career lately and more interested in his relic hunting hobby. I guess Carl thought Frank would look at the generous offer as a good thing. That maybe he'd start doing dentistry part time at someone else's practice."

Holly leaned in a little. "You know, I think I was mostly out of the loop in terms of how devoted Frank was to relic hunting. I thought it was just something he did on the side, every once in a while. Do you know much about that?"

Lindy gave a small smile. "That's something I really loved about Frank. His eyes would light up when he started talking about history. That's what relic hunting was to him—history coming to life. He was sort of shy at first when he was mentioning it to me. I guess he thought I might not be interested."

"Lots of people weren't," said Holly wryly. "I have the feeling that's why Frank didn't talk about it with me much. He thought I wouldn't be interested, or that I wouldn't be very receptive to hearing about it."

"Right. That's why I think he wasn't saying much to me about it, either, at first. But then, as I asked more questions about it and asked to come along with him to a site, he started talking about it more and more."

Holly gave her a sad smile. "*Were* you interested? Or were you trying to show interest in the things Frank liked?"

"No, I was genuinely interested in it. I was a history minor in college. The artifacts that Frank found were fascinating to me. Anyway, he spent more and more time on his computer looking at prospective sites. And he'd head over to the library, of course, to look at the Sanborn maps." Her voice broke at the mention of the library.

We were quiet for a few moments to help Lindy regain control. She took a deep breath and continued evenly, "Frank was also writing articles about his finds. He was getting to be recognized as a genuine expert. I think that made him the proudest of anything. Businesses and property owners were reaching out to him first when they were interested in developing sites."

Holly said, "I know that made him happy. It's great to get recognition, especially when you've been working as hard as Frank was."

Lindy nodded. "He was definitely happy about it. But lately, there was something on Frank's mind. He was very preoccupied with one of the digs he was on."

"Even more preoccupied than usual?" asked Holly.

"I guess preoccupied in a *bad* way, instead of a good way. Usually, it was almost like a treasure hunt for him. He loved all the different tools he was using and the research. But in the last week or so, he seemed more worried about the dig. When I'd ask him how things were going, he would clam up instead of chatting about it."

Holly frowned. "That doesn't sound like him. Was there anything else on his mind?" She gave a short laugh. "Stupid question. It sounds like there was a lot of stuff going on at work that was on his mind. The potential sale of the practice where he worked."

"Yes, but that wasn't the only thing. He was also worried about something else. Something he wasn't willing to share with me yet. He was talking really vaguely about friendship and what it meant to be a good friend. He asked me one night if there were limits to friendship."

Holly stilled. "So he was talking about his friendship with Paul. His best friend."

"I'm not positive he was talking about the mayor. He might have been thinking about Carl, who's just a work friend. Maybe he was feeling guilty about not allowing Carl to sell the practice and move to be with his mother. Or maybe he was thinking about Warner."

Holly frowned. "The other relic hunter?"

Lindy nodded. "Frank didn't really view Warner as competition for sites, although I know Warner did. They'd started arguing a lot lately. Frank had been complaining about him. Maybe Frank thought he should make sure Warner had some good sites. He could have been wondering if he should give Warner the site he'd been planning on working." Lindy gave a short laugh. "And maybe I'm just grasping at straws. I can't figure out who would want to kill Frank. I wish I'd known that he had so much on his mind. I wish I'd listened to him more."

"None of this is your fault, Lindy," said Holly. "Remember that. The only person is responsible is the one who did this to Frank."

Lindy nodded, seeming to tear up again. Holly changed the subject, and they chatted for a few minutes longer before Holly and I headed out.

Chapter Twelve

"Thanks for going with me to see Lindy," said Holly when we were back in her car. "I think I needed the moral support for some reason. I just didn't want to head over there by myself."

"Of course you didn't," I said. "I'm happy to do anything I can to help you out." I hesitated. "Are your parents going to help you tackle Frank's things?"

Holly shook her head. "No, they already mentioned that they thought it would be too hard on them. I think they're barely holding on as it is."

I said tentatively, "If you're wanting to start the process, I'd be glad to help. I didn't know if it's something you'd rather put off or not. I know having some time pass might make it easier."

"Actually, I was thinking about going ahead and getting started. It's sort of like ripping off a bandage," Holly said wryly. "Sometimes it's better to just get it over with. And I'd love the help."

We went back to the house to find Grayson at the kitchen table on his laptop. He gave us a rueful smile. "Couldn't stop myself from doing a little work."

I raised an eyebrow at him. "And you thought that *I'd* be the one who'd get pulled back into work?"

Grayson blushed, which made me smile. He said, "Yeah, I know. I guess the problem with taking a break is that you and I both love our jobs." He glanced over at Holly. "How did the visit with Lindy go?"

"It was good, thanks," she said. "It wasn't as awkward as I thought it might be." Holly glanced over at me. "I'm going to go change real quick. I have the feeling we might encounter some dust."

As Holly went upstairs, I slid into the chair next to Grayson. "You're okay to work for a while?"

"Sure thing. If I get tired of it, I can always play games online with Jeremy. He's playing online now, even though it's a workday." Grayson grinned. "I have the feeling this job of his isn't long for this world." His smile faded when he saw how distracted I was looking. "Everything okay?"

"Yes, it's good. I'm going to help Holly clear out Frank's house. Just help get her started, you know. I need to change, too."

Fitz padded down the stairs and gave me a serious look. I wondered if he could feel some of the tension in the house following Frank's death. Animals were always so good at picking up on nuances. I reached down and scratched him under his chin until I could hear him purring, his eyes nearly shut.

"Sounds good. Then, do you want to go out and grab something to eat? We can invite Holly or bring food back for her."

I said, "Perfect." Then I hurried upstairs to put some of my grungier workout clothes on.

Fifteen minutes later, we were at Frank's house. Holly pulled into the long driveway. I could see where Frank would have fit in well in the house. It was a two-story design with a graceful porch and large windows to soak in the natural light. The yard was neatly manicured and sported flowerbeds bursting with color. I wondered if June had been the gardener. Part of me thought she might be, but the meticulous upkeep of the yard seemed to point to Frank, despite his lack of time. When Holly used her key to let us inside, I saw a tastefully decorated interior with a plush sofa and soft throw pillows.

The house was cheerful but already felt a little abandoned. I thought I was just being fanciful, but then I saw Holly shiver and knew she felt the same way. Plus, there were signs the police had been through the house. I was sure they'd probably taken Frank's computers to look for clues to his death.

"Where do you want to start?" I asked her.

Holly was looking around, her hands on her hips. She sighed. "I guess clothing would be an easy way to hop into it. It's just going to be a matter of pulling it out and giving it away."

We hopped into it. When we went upstairs, and Holly opened Frank's closet doors, I saw rows of clothing sorted by color.

"Wow," I said, impressed. I gave Holly an apologetic smile. "Sorry. I'm just not used to seeing men be this neat. I mean, Grayson is pretty organized at his house, but it's nothing compared to this. And Grayson's office is totally chaotic."

Holly chuckled. "Yeah. June never had to worry about picking up discarded socks off the floor. Frank was always a neat freak. I remember wondering how he survived being in a college dorm. Whoever his roommate was probably drove Frank crazy with his sloppiness."

We ended up making a couple of trips to the Goodwill store to drop off all of Frank's clothing and shoes. His clothes all looked nice; even the clothing that I'd supposed he'd used for his relic hunting.

When we got back to the house, Holly said, "I think we should look through Frank's desk. I know the cops went through everything, but maybe there's something there that would mean something to me that didn't seem significant to them."

"Sure," I said. "It'll be a straightforward job, especially if Frank's desk looks like his closet did."

And of course, it did. Again, there was evidence the police had rifled through the desk. Even the slightest bit of disorganization, I attributed to the police having searched it. Frank was just too tidy to leave his desk anything other than pristine.

Holly pulled out a composition book from a desk drawer and opened it. She turned the pages carefully, looking down rows of Frank's neat, careful handwriting. "This is apparently where he logged the different sites he was working at," she said slowly. "He wrote the address and made notes as to any finds that were located."

"Was there anything listed about the most recent site?" I asked.

Holly handed me the composition notebook. I saw an unfamiliar address and then the words *human remains*. We looked at each other.

"I'm sure finding human remains, even historic ones, would probably mean the police would have to be involved," I said.

"That's what I'm thinking. And wouldn't it mean that any sort of development would have to be put on hold? It could be an entire cemetery, for all they know. Charleston dates back to the late 1600s."

"I bet Warner would know," I said.

Holly was already pulling her phone out. She dialed his number and then put the phone on speaker.

Warner answered his phone, sounding a little peeved. "Hello?"

"Warner? This is Holly."

Warner underwent a quick attitude adjustment, although I could tell there was still some irritation underneath. "Oh, hi, Holly. Uh, everything okay?"

It was a testament to Warner's social ineptitude that he would ask a grieving sister that question.

Holly quickly said, "I'm holding up, thanks. Listen, Ann and I are over at Frank's house, doing some clearing out. I just went through his desk and found a notebook where he logged the different sites he'd been working on."

The mention of relic hunting seemed to spark Warner's interest. "Did you? I had the feeling Frank would be super-organized with that stuff." He paused. "I'd love to look at the notebook sometime."

"Sure. Maybe after we get everything settled here. I had a quick question for you about the site Frank was working on when he died," said Holly.

"I didn't really know anything about that site. Frank sometimes didn't share information." The peeved tone had worked its way back into Warner's voice.

"That's fine. I've got Frank's notes on it. But it sounds like he found human remains at the site."

There was another pause on the other end. "*Did* he?"

"Holly and I were wondering what that would mean," I said, "in terms of the development."

"Well, it would bring everything to a crashing halt," said Warner, sounding a little excited. "If it was a business, they'd have to put all their plans for the development on hold until the site was fully investigated. That could mean that the building materials they'd budgeted for and the labor they'd hired would increase dramatically in cost."

"What if it's a private individual?" asked Holly.

"Well, it would do the same thing. If it's supposed to be someone's new home, that house is going to be delayed by a long while. The police would have to come in, but there would also need to be more relic hunters to determine if the remains were part of a private or public cemetery. A discovery of human remains changes everything."

"Got it," said Holly. "Ann and I thought that it probably would, but I wanted to bounce it off you. Thanks."

"And the notebook?" Warner squeaked.

"I'll call you later about it."

Holly hung up, and we looked at each other. I said, "I wonder if the police realized the implications of this notebook."

"I'm thinking they didn't, because surely they'd have taken it with them. I'm going to give that lieutenant a call." She looked through her contact list and made the call.

"Roberts," a voice answered immediately.

"Lieutenant Roberts?" asked Holly. "Hi. It's Holly Walsh."

"Ms. Walsh. What can I help you with?"

Holly said, "I was just over at my brother's house, clearing out some of his things. I was wondering if you'd taken a close look at his notebook."

Roberts hesitated. "The composition notebook that was in his desk?"

"That's right. According to his notes, he found human remains at the site he was working on. I just wanted to make sure you were aware of that."

Roberts said, "Thanks for checking in. We actually were aware of that and took pictures of the notebook. We're following up on that and other leads."

"Good." Holly paused. "Have you found anything out yet?"

Roberts's voice was less-brisk now and gentler. "Nothing I can divulge right now. I'm sorry. But please know that we're giving this case all our attention."

"Thank you," said Holly, and hung up.

Holly and I looked at each other for a few minutes. Then Holly rubbed her temples as if her head hurt. "This is all a lot."

"Do you want to take a break from cleaning?" I asked. "I can come back with you any time."

"Yeah, let's do that. The clothes were easy. The desk items and Frank's furniture and things like that are going to be way harder." Holly glanced down at her phone, which had just gone off. "Plus, it looks like Mom and Dad are on their way down. I guess they headed here early. They're probably having just as hard of a time sitting still as I am. I feel like I'm more in control of the situation when I'm actually *doing* something, even if it's just cleaning stuff up."

We headed back to Holly's house. She delved right back into the memorial service planning, and Grayson and I slipped out the door with waves when she was on the phone. She gave us an absent wave in return.

"How did that go?" asked Grayson, when we were in the car together. "I'm thinking it could be a very emotional process, going through your brother's things."

"She did great," I said. "We worked through a lot of stuff and had a huge amount of nice clothes to give away. It was when we started going through Frank's desk that things started going sideways."

Grayson lifted his eyebrows. "Did you find something?"

"Maybe. But Frank had a log of all the sites he'd worked on and notes regarding the discoveries. We found out that he'd discovered human remains at the site he's working on now."

Grayson's eyes opened wide. "No way."

"Apparently, it's not as rare as you'd think. Charleston is such an old city, by US standards, anyway. Whenever you discover human remains, all construction work is delayed, of course. Or, I guess, possibly even canceled for good, depending on exactly what is uncovered."

Grayson said, "Sure. If it indicates a major historic find." He gave a low whistle. "So maybe the reason Frank was murdered was because someone didn't want him to disclose his discovery. So that the development could continue."

I nodded. "Someone could have followed him, looking for a moment to catch Frank alone. The library was risky, but possibly not as risky as allowing Frank to stop the construction."

"Did Holly tell the police what the two of you found?"

I nodded again. "Right away. It sounded like they were already aware of it. I'm sure the police can figure out who's behind the development at the site. It wasn't something that was listed in Frank's notebook. It just listed the site address."

My head was swimming with all the information we'd gathered from the last couple of days. I might have looked overwhelmed because before I knew it, Grayson had whisked me away into a restaurant. "My treat," he said. And, over the course of the meal and some wine, I felt some of the stress melt away.

Chapter Thirteen

The next day passed quietly by. I helped Holly make a few follow-up phone calls to finalize the memorial plans. Grayson and I greeted Holly's parents when they arrived, and they gave me a warm hug and thanked me for being there for Holly.

Then the morning of the memorial service was upon us. Holly had outlawed wearing black, instead encouraging everyone to wear cheerful colors that made it clear that we were indeed celebrating Frank's life. The funeral home was decorated with an array of cheerful flowers. There were several smiling photos of Frank; Frank with family, with friends, and even one of him investigating a site. Several friends gave readings from favorite books and poetry, and a guitarist played one of Frank's favorite songs. The service really engendered a connection with Frank's legacy . . . such a connection that it almost felt as if he were there with us.

Lindy Baker was there, sitting with the family and looking pale and tired. I saw her give a faint, reminiscent smile a couple of times during the service.

Holly had noticed Carl Hopkins, Frank's dental partner, was there shortly before the service started. He looked a little uncomfortable about being there as the service was wrapping up. He was someone I definitely wanted to talk to, and I wasn't sure I was going to have another opportunity. Plus, Holly was going to be swamped with people wanting to extend their condolences. I was worried Carl might try to slip out the door without speaking to anyone. I made it my mission to make sure that didn't happen.

When I murmured my plan to Grayson, he glanced across the room at Carl, and then nodded at me. I smiled. Grayson had an excellent way of getting people to talk to him. It must have been a reporter's instinct. Or maybe it was just his outgoing personality and the fact that people liked him.

Sure enough, it looked as if Carl was working his way to the exit, through the throng of people. I hurried to catch up with him, Grayson right behind me.

I wasn't entirely sure what my plan was or how to stop the train that was Carl Hopkins. He seemed determined to make it to his car. I hoped Grayson had a good idea because otherwise, the two of us were going to look a little crazy.

Fortunately for us, Carl was in such a hurry that he stumbled down the short flight of stairs, taking a tumble to the ground. His face was stormy.

"Need a hand?" asked Grayson smoothly.

Carl looked up at him, bemusedly. "What? Oh. No, I'm all right."

But when he tried to stand up, his ankle didn't cooperate. Carl cursed under his breath. "Must have twisted the stupid thing."

"Do you need us to drive you to an urgent care?" I asked.

Carl irritably shook his head. "No, I just need to rest it for a minute. Of all the luck."

Grayson urged, "Let us help you over to that bench over there."

Reluctantly, Carl allowed Grayson to heave him up and help him over to the bench. Carl plopped down and glared at the stairs that had put him in this predicament.

"I'll grab some ice from inside," said Grayson.

Before Carl could stop him, Grayson took off. Carl sighed. Then he looked at me, seeming awkward. "Friend of Frank's?" he asked.

I said, "I knew Frank a little, but I'm mainly here to support Holly. I was her college roommate." I held out my hand. "Ann Beckett."

He shook it, muttered out his own name a bit ungraciously.

I said brightly, "Oh, you're Frank's dental partner. Holly mentioned Frank said nice things about you."

Carl looked a little suspicious, as if disbelieving that Frank would have done such a thing. "Hm."

Fortunately, Grayson returned with a zipper bag of ice. Carl took it from him and cradled it against his damaged ankle.

Grayson said in his easy voice, "Almost like Cinderella trying to get away from the ball. Do you have an appointment you need to get to?"

Carl looked at him with dislike. "No." He paused, looking at me. "Did Holly really mention that Frank had good things to say about me?"

"Of course." I didn't actually know this, but I was hoping Carl would elaborate just a little more about his relationship with Frank.

Carl's expression grew a little brighter. "That's good to hear. I've been feeling strange about being here. Frank and I ordinarily got on well together. He was easy to work with—good to communicate about various things, always did his work, arrived promptly, and he was fairly cheerful in the office."

"But the two of you had issues lately?" I asked.

Carl looked at me sharply. "Why would you think that?"

"Because you were bolting out of here to leave the service."

Carl sighed. "Right. Yes, I was trying to get out of here. I felt really strongly that I needed to attend to pay my respects. But I didn't want to speak with the family in case they felt badly about Frank and me having a falling out." He rolled his eyes. "The police apparently already have me pegged as the person who killed him."

Grayson frowned. "What makes you think that?"

"Oh, I don't know. Because Frank and I had had words, I guess." Carl's expression relaxed for a moment. "Although I gave the cops an alibi, so they probably don't consider me much of a suspect, after all. I told them I was in the office when Frank died."

I saw some movement out of the corner of my eye and saw Lindy Baker, Carl's receptionist, coming up from behind the bench. She froze, looking startled. By what, I wasn't sure.

A moment later, she called out, "Carl? Are you okay?"

Carl tried to turn around, but then Lindy came around the front of the bench. Carl looked even more aggravated than he had before. I guessed he was the type of person who didn't enjoy showing much weakness. In a grouchy voice, he said, "I'm okay. I just twisted my ankle coming down the stairs, that's all."

"Good," said Lindy with a small smile. "I spotted the bag of ice and was worried."

Carl didn't seem enthused about carrying on a conversation with his receptionist/bookkeeper. Lindy quickly said, "Well, I better go find Holly's parents. I wanted to speak with them before I go." She slipped quietly away.

Carl relaxed a little after she left.

"What was the falling-out about?" asked Grayson in a casual voice.

Carl stared at him blankly.

"You'd said you and Frank had a falling-out and you felt uncomfortable about being here," reminded Grayson.

"Oh, that," said Carl. He shrugged. "It's a sort of long story."

"I don't think you're going anywhere anytime soon," said Grayson, gesturing at Carl's ankle, which had swollen up.

"Maybe it's broken," I said.

Carl shot me a look. "It's fine. I do have a medical background."

Grayson raised an eyebrow at me as if to say, "can you believe this guy?"

Carl cleared his throat. "It wasn't much of a falling-out. Mostly just a difference of opinion, that's all. And, probably, it also has to do with the fact that Frank and I were at different stages of our lives." He suddenly stopped short, as if it just occurred to him that Frank would not continue to progress to another stage. He sighed. "It wasn't a huge age difference. Just ten years or so. But my parents had me late in life. My dad is alive, but is suffering from advanced dementia. Then my mother started having health problems. Plus, she's not the kind of person who likes to be alone. And she never had a big support network of friends up there. My dad was her whole world."

I said, "I can understand why you'd want to go up there to be with her. And to see your dad, of course."

Carl shook his head. "I don't even think I *want* to go up there. But I feel a sense of responsibility to my mother. And, to be honest, I feel that responsibility because of my dad, too. It's what *he* would have wanted me to do; take care of Mom. And even though he's mentally gone now, I still feel indebted to him. To both of them, really."

Grayson said, "But to give up your dental practice? That's got to be a pretty big deal, right? Is it going to be easy to set up shop in another state? To find a practice to join or start one of your own? All while you're trying to take care of your mom?"

It was exactly what I'd been thinking. But Grayson's voice was laced with concern, as if he was genuinely worried about Carl and what he faced when he moved. Maybe he was. Once again, I admired Grayson's innate skill in making people talk about uncomfortable subjects.

I could tell Carl was eating up the attention, too. He leaned forward. "I'm not even all that sure I want to be a dentist anymore, to be honest. I've never found it all that rewarding. Whenever I'm spending time with a patient, I'm filling cavities or doing root canals." Even mentioning it made Carl look tired.

I said, "But you're helping them, too. They're coming in with a painful problem, and you're fixing the issue."

Carl shrugged. "I'm not sure the patients really see it that way. They all avoid coming in. They'll reschedule appointments several times. I don't know—maybe I'm simply having a midlife crisis and simply want to try something new. Moving sounds like an adventure to me, instead of a lot of work. It means making new connections, having a new neighborhood, maybe exploring a new career or hobbies. I'm starting to really look at what it means to be successful."

"You don't feel successful now?" I asked. He was a man who definitely had all the trappings of success. But there was a haunted look on his face, as if he wasn't happy at all and hadn't been for a long time.

He shook his head. "Not really. Professionally? Sure. But not in a meaningful way. Look at my love life, or lack of it. I've never been able to marry. I can't meet anybody because all I'm doing is going to work and coming back home again. This town is cliquey, too, which doesn't help. Also, I feel like I'm burned out."

"Lots of long hours at work?" asked Grayson sympathetically.

"Lots. But it's more than that. I feel like I've been in a real slog for the last twenty years. School was tough, and I never went out because I needed to stay inside and study. Work hasn't exactly been easy, either." He chuckled. "I've been thinking that what I really need is a gap year. I know that's something kids do before they go to college, but it's something I could use, too. A year off to explore the world before delving right back into working. I could take my mom along with me. She always enjoyed traveling."

"Sounds like a great idea," I said.

Carl nodded. "If it works out." He paused. "You know, Frank was coming around to the idea of selling the practice. He could tell we'd gotten a great offer for it. Frank was even thinking about setting up a solo practice of his own. I told him I thought that would be a wonderful idea. He could be his own boss."

This sounded like wishful thinking. From what I'd heard, Frank had no intention of selling the practice, great offer or not. In a lot of ways, he'd sounded more like Carl—burned out on work and not that invested in being a dentist. Frank hadn't sounded like someone who wanted to be his own boss. People who owned their own business are usually at work all the time. He'd sounded like someone who wanted to pursue his passion for relic hunting, even if it meant spending less time at his practice.

Carl winced again, perhaps once again realizing that Frank was gone, and his future was no longer in question. "It's just so hard to believe this happened to him," he muttered.

"How had Frank seemed lately?" I asked.

"Preoccupied," said Carl immediately. "Frank didn't seem like he was totally on his game. If he hadn't been such a good dentist, I'd have been worried about his patients. But for Frank, excellent dentistry was muscle memory. He could have a lot on his mind and still take care of his patients at the same time."

"Any idea what might have been on his mind?" asked Grayson.

Carl's eyes scanned the people coming out the door. "Yes. I overheard him on the phone talking about one of his digs. He said something about having found human remains."

To our credit, Grayson and I acted as if this was the first time we'd heard about this. Carl continued, "The problem was that a good friend of his was involved in the development of the site."

"The mayor?" I breathed out.

Carl looked surprised that I'd have guessed that. Then he said, "I guess you've known Frank a long time. Yes, the mayor apparently had some sort of stake in the development of the property. Finding old buttons or belt buckles is one thing. Finding bones is another. The whole project might have to be scuttled."

Grayson gave a low whistle.

"Exactly," said Carl. "Paul would stand to lose a lot of money if the development didn't go through. I called a cop friend of mine here. Acquaintance, I should say. He's one of my patients. I filled him in on the conversation I'd overheard. To my relief, the police already knew about it. They're apparently starting to poke around and see if there might be an ethics violation."

Grayson said, "Well, if the mayor murdered Frank to cover up what he'd discovered, I'd say that would be a pretty big ethics violation."

"Oh, of course. But it could go even deeper. It sounds like the mayor might have pushed for the development to be approved because he had a stake in its success. Paul could get into a lot of trouble for that."

I asked, "Did the police say how ethics violations are handled?"

"The cop told me, just vaguely because he said he couldn't be specific, that different things could happen. The state would have to decide how egregious Paul's misconduct was and what harm he might have caused. He could be fined or just censured. On the other hand, he could be removed from office or even imprisoned."

Maybe that was why Paul had seemed so grim the night of his engagement party. Not only was he grieving the death of his best friend, he was also facing the fact that not only might he be on the cusp of losing a great deal of money, he might also be in a lot of trouble. Could it be even worse? Could some of his grimness result from guilt? For having killed his friend?

Carl glanced at his watch. "I should get going."

"Hold up," said Grayson. "You need to check your ankle first. Make sure you can put some weight on it."

I could tell that's the last thing Carl wanted to do. It looked like he was ready to speed away. But he listened and then a few moments later, Carl gently put pressure on his leg and foot. With a satisfied smile, he said, "It's fine. I just wrenched it, as I thought. All I needed was to sit down and rest it for a few minutes. Nice to meet you both."

He hurried away for the parking lot without turning back.

Chapter Fourteen

Grayson said in a low voice, "Well, he was intense."

I nodded. "My thoughts exactly."

I saw Lindy standing outside, her arms wrapped around herself, although the weather was humid. She was staring toward the departing Carl.

Grayson and I walked back toward the funeral home. I introduced Grayson to Lindy.

"Are you holding up okay?" I asked her.

Her gaze was still following Carl, now pulling out of the parking lot. She gave a small shrug of a thin shoulder. "I guess. But I can tell you one thing; if Carl doesn't sell the business soon, I'm going to find a new job. I don't want to work for him anymore."

Grayson and I exchanged a quick glance. "Is he tough to work for?"

"He's just very intense," said Lindy. "Ordinarily, he's not so bad. He's not particularly friendly to me, but he's polite. He always gets his work done, even though I get the feeling he doesn't really enjoy his job. But the main problem right now is that I don't trust him."

I dropped my voice. "You think he has something to do with Frank's death?"

Lindy didn't lower her voice and her tone was full of indignation. "I heard him say he was at the office when Frank died. Absolutely not true. He was in and out of the office that morning. Plus, I don't think he ever even liked Frank. Their personalities were like oil and water. When this stuff about selling the practice came up, it was even worse. I could tell Frank was avoiding Carl. I was, too. Carl was getting more and more intense and brooding more and more. It was like a heavy cloud in the building. And today? He looked more cheerful than I've seen him in a long time, even though he's at a *funeral*. And injured himself on the way out the door! I bet he's already accepted the offer to sell the practice."

Lindy stopped, shaking her head. "Sorry. You didn't need to hear me rant today. I think I need to get out of here. Go lie down for a while."

"That's a good idea," I said. "You've got to be exhausted. Are you going to take some time off work?"

"Probably. But I need to go in tomorrow morning to take care of some things first. I'll just arrive super-early so I won't have to be pleasant to Carl," said Lindy grimly. "I'll see you two later."

As she walked toward the parking lot, I couldn't help but feel as if she'd been holding something back.

When we walked back inside the funeral home, we found that many of the mourners had finished speaking with the family and were on their way out. Holly spotted Grayson and me and waved us over to where her mother and father were standing. Susan and Ira looked much the same from when I'd known them in college, although now signs of stress lined their faces and their eyes were red. Holly introduced Grayson to them and they gave him a weary smile.

Holly's folks reached out to hug me tightly. "I'm so sorry," I murmured to them.

"We just can't believe it," said Ira, his voice breaking.

Susan gave me a pleading look, as if I could somehow explain it in a way that made sense to them. "We spoke to him the night before he died. He sounded like everything was fine. Who could have done something like this? We thought everybody liked Frank."

"Maybe it was just a random accident," said Ira, eager to grasp at straws. "Somebody just stumbled and hit the bookcases hard. Then ran away when he saw what had happened so he wouldn't get into trouble."

Holly glanced at us with tears in her eyes, knowing her dad was trying to make things seem better than they actually were. But I nodded, and Grayson did, too.

Ira looked relieved that we'd approved of his unlikely scenario.

"Enough of all this," said Susan quietly. "I don't believe I can think about Frank's death another moment without losing my mind. We've spoken to everyone. Let's go out and have a nice lunch. I want to get caught up with Ann and learn more about Grayson."

"A lunch with drinks," said Ira with a sigh. "Drinks are definitely going to be required." He glanced at us and said gruffly, "And everything is on us. I don't want to hear a word otherwise. And we're going to have a delightful time." It was a tone that brooked no argument.

I knew Ira was a force to be reckoned with. He was definitely a man used to getting his own way. He must be hating the feeling of being out of control regarding Frank's death. Holly had mentioned to me that Ira had insisted on meeting with the police to get updates. Unfortunately, they'd had to hold details of the investigation close to their chests. It must be very frustrating for him.

Surprisingly, it was exactly as Ira had commanded: we *did* have a good time. Part of this was because the family came up with a bunch of funny Frank stories, which put us all in gales of laughter. We ate great seafood at a downtown restaurant, watching as Ira and Susan put away tons of food. They also put away a great deal of alcohol—enough that Holly asked me to drive her car while she drove her parents to their hotel. We followed and took Holly back to her place.

"Whew," said Holly, as we got out and walked up the walkway to her house. "That was tiring. But somehow, not as bad as I thought it would be, you know? It was hard, but it ended up being exactly what we'd wanted: a celebration of life. I think Frank would have liked what we did."

"I'm sure he would have," I said.

Holly was fishing out her house keys when I glanced up at the windows and chuckled.

Grayson followed my gaze. "Looks like we have a welcoming committee," he said, grinning.

Sure enough, a golden retriever's excited face was smiling at us from one window and an orange cat's from another.

"It's nice to have someone who's thrilled when you walk in the door," said Holly, laughing herself.

Murphy nearly bowled us over when we opened the door. He bounced around like he was Tigger. Fitz, in a much quieter way, was just as delighted to see us. He brushed against all our legs.

Grayson said, "I'll take Murphy for a walk and then play ball with him in the backyard."

Holly gave him a grateful look. "You're now officially my favorite person ever. I love Murphy, but right this second, I just don't think I can summon the energy to handle him."

Murphy had the wiggles as soon as Grayson had mentioned the magic words "walk" and "ball," and it was tricky to put his harness on him. But soon, he bounded out the door with Grayson behind him.

Holly kicked off her shoes and stretched out on the sofa. "He's the best, you know. Grayson, I mean, not Murphy."

"I don't know. I think Murphy is probably the best, too," I said in a teasing voice.

"Are you and Grayson serious?" asked Holly, raising her eyebrows. "Tell me if I'm getting too nosy."

"We really like each other," I said. "And I think we've decided we'll see where that takes us."

"Good idea," said Holly, trying to suppress a yawn. "Now I just need to find somebody. It's not so easy."

"We talked to Carl today at the funeral," I said. "He mentioned Charleston could be a tough place to meet people. I think the word he used was 'cliquey.'"

"He's not wrong," said Holly with a shrug. She stretched. "Did you get any information from Carl? I'd love something else to share with the police. Every day that goes by, it makes me think justice won't be meted out for Frank's death."

"I guess the process of investigation takes a while. But Grayson and I did talk with Carl. He's thinking about stepping away from dentistry."

Holly's eyes opened wide. "Really? Boy, that sounds like a major midlife crisis, if I ever heard one. I mean, you go to all that expensive school, put yourself through all the hard work and the studying? Then you get out of it?"

"I know. I don't think he's totally decided on that, but it definitely sounded like it was a possibility." I paused. "The bombshell, though, was about Frank's site."

"The most recent one? The one he was researching when he died?" Holly's voice was tight.

"That's right. He said the site Frank was digging on was a development the mayor was involved with."

Holly seemed to stop breathing for a few moments. "You mean Paul had a stake in the development? Then Frank found human remains there?"

I nodded. "According to Carl."

We were quiet for a minute while Holly absorbed this information. Then she said, "So you're saying that Paul, first off, may have been unethically involved in this development. Following that train of thought, though, let's assume Frank felt really conflicted when he realized there were human remains on the site. He knows the site is important to Paul. Paul is his best friend. Maybe he calls Paul on the phone to let him know what he's found. We heard from Lindy that Frank had been ruminating a lot on friendship lately. Maybe he was thinking about his friendship with Paul."

"What do you think Paul would have said?" I asked.

Holly blew out her breath. "Well, he sure wouldn't have been happy about it. Paul was always motivated by money. I'm sure he would have tried to keep Frank quiet."

"And what would Frank have done after being told to keep quiet?"

Holly shook her head. "It would have bothered the stew out of him. He'd have been worrying about it day and night. Because one thing Frank was, was ethical. Maybe he told Paul that he could keep quiet about the discovery for a little while until Paul figured out what he needed to do. But Frank wouldn't have sat on the information forever. He'd have been pushing the envelope with Paul, prodding him to reveal what he'd discovered."

I said slowly, "Do you think Paul could have killed Frank? To keep him silent?"

Holly looked ill. "I really hope not. They were like brothers. I can't really imagine Paul doing that. But then, if he felt like he was being pushed into a corner, maybe he did. I mean, it wouldn't just mean the end of a lucrative development. It might mean that his whole connection with the development went public. That he would be up on an ethics violation."

"Do you think Frank knew Paul's involvement with the development wasn't ethical?" I asked.

"I doubt it. Frank didn't pay attention to that sort of thing. He would have just been looking at the site as a place to dig and relic hunt. He wasn't going to do any sort of provenance on the site. He probably took it all at face value. If Frank had believed there was any sort of funny business going on, he'd have gone right to the cops, friend or no friend. Like I said, he was ethical. But he could also be clueless." Holly sighed. "It's a lot to think about."

I felt instantly guilty. "Sorry, I didn't mean to dump that stuff on you right after your brother's funeral. You were already exhausted."

"No, it's fine. I *wanted* to know."

I nodded.

Chapter Fifteen

The next morning, I heard Holly downstairs early. It sounded like she was organizing things; putting things into drawers, cabinets, and closets. I knew she'd taken back a small pile of stuff from Frank's house. I felt like I needed to get up and see if I could give her a hand.

Grayson was still asleep, and when I went downstairs, I saw that Holly's golden retriever was still looking sleepy, too. Murphy's tail knocked on the floor a few times in greeting, but he was too tired to raise his head.

Holly snorted. "Grayson sure did a good job wearing Murphy out yesterday. He must have walked for miles. And then played ball on top of that."

"Grayson did a good job wearing *himself* out, too," I said wryly. I gestured to the pile of photos and other memorabilia in front of Holly on the kitchen table. "Can I give you a hand with any of that?"

Holly shook her head. "I just wanted to take a quick glance through them. I've already put some other stuff away. I flipped through a few of the pictures when we were at Frank's house, and grabbed the whole stack because I thought they looked like they might be good. There's a great picture of Frank and Lindy in there."

She held it out for me to see. Frank was grinning more than I'd ever seen him grin. Lindy looked happy too, a broad smile stretching over her pretty features.

Holly said, "Want to run this by the dental office with me? Grayson, too, if he's up for it. I thought it might be a good excuse for me to see Carl and maybe ask a few follow-up questions. Especially since he bolted out of the funeral service like the hounds of hell were after him. Why do you think he was so eager to escape?"

"He seemed to feel really uncomfortable. Maybe because he and Frank weren't really getting along as well as they had been."

"Which is exactly why I'd like to talk to him," said Holly grimly.

"I briefly spoke to Lindy yesterday, too. She said she was going to quit her job—something she hasn't told Carl yet. Anyway, she's running by the office early this morning to get some stuff done. Maybe even to collect her things, since it didn't sound like she was going to give two weeks' notice. So now might be a good time to see her."

Holly nodded. "And Grayson?"

"I'm thinking he could use the sleep."

A few minutes later, we set out. Holly was in a quiet, tense mood, so I was quiet too, letting her mull over her thoughts. Whatever they were, they were clearly troubling her, judging from the frown on her face.

We pulled up to the dental office. "Looks like Carl isn't here yet," said Holly, "but that's Lindy's car. She's here early, like you said. We can always grab coffee after we see Lindy and lurk until Carl shows up."

We walked into the office, which was unlocked. It was silent inside.

"Lindy?" called Holly. "It's Holly and Ann."

There was no response.

"Maybe she's in the restroom or something," I said.

But Holly seemed increasingly anxious. "Lindy?" she called again.

No answer.

Lindy had clearly been working—there were papers on her desk. Holly went straight through to the exam rooms, sticking her head in each one and calling for Lindy.

I went to the restroom and saw no one in it. On my way back out, I saw something on the floor behind the reception desk. Feeling a cold fissure up my spine, I cautiously craned my head until I saw what I feared I'd see.

Lindy Baker was sprawled behind her desk, lying in a pool of blood.

Chapter Sixteen

Lindy's eyes were open, staring blankly at the ceiling. It looked like she'd been hit by a heavy object right on her forehead, but I couldn't see what the weapon might have been.

"Holly!" I called out.

When she appeared from the back of the building, I said, "Don't come any closer, so we protect the area." I didn't say crime scene, but that was clearly what it was. I reached out a trembling hand to Lindy's neck. I glanced up to meet Holly's questioning look. I shook my head.

Holly clapped her hand over her mouth, eyes wide.

"Let's get out of the building," I whispered.

I used a tissue to open the door, and we stepped outside, both of us gasping for air as if we'd been running.

It seemed like it took the better part of an hour for the police to get there, but I realized later it must have been fewer than fifteen minutes. While we waited, Holly paced nervously at the sidewalk. "What is going on? First Frank, now Lindy? Do you think it was a burglary or something? Something unrelated?"

I shook my head. "I kind of doubt it. It seems too coincidental." I reached out and gave Holly a hug, and she gave a small sob. "I'm so sorry."

The police finally pulled up, sirens wailing and lights flashing. An ambulance did the same. I looked sadly at the ambulance, knowing there was no one in there to save, only to transport.

One of the officers came over to ask Holly and me to stay where we were. Others went inside. A minute later, they were out again, stringing up crime scene tape while Holly and I watched mutely.

We were sitting on the curb by the time the police came over to speak with us. One of the younger cops gave us a sympathetic look. "Lieutenant Roberts is on his way over and wants to speak with both of you. Want to sit over there instead?" He gestured to a set of stairs to another business. The steps were in the shade. "You might be more comfortable. It's getting hot out here."

Holly and I took him up on it. It was another fifteen minutes before Lt. Roberts arrived, went briefly inside, and then came back out to talk to us.

"How are you doing?" he asked.

It was a good way to open. I was sure Holly and I both looked tired and stressed. I'd thought he might begin by asking us what we'd been doing there. The kindness in his voice made tears slowly streak down Holly's face.

"We're okay," she said finally in a tight voice. "Better than Lindy, anyway."

Maybe Holly anticipated his next question because she pulled the photo out of her tote bag of a purse. "We were here to give Lindy this."

The lieutenant took the photo from us, studying it carefully.

"I found it when Ann and I were cleaning out Frank's place. I thought she might want it." Holly impatiently swiped at a tear.

Roberts nodded. "Was Lindy usually at the office this early?"

Holly shrugged a shoulder and glanced at me.

I cleared my throat. "I saw Lindy at the memorial service yesterday. She mentioned she didn't want to work here anymore, but that she was planning on coming in early today to wrap some things up. When Holly mentioned bringing Lindy the photo, I thought we should run by early to make sure we caught her before she left."

"Which we didn't do," choked out Holly.

Roberts took in a deep breath. "I'm very sorry you had to find her like that. Can you tell me about coming into the building? Were the doors open? Unlocked? Did you notice anything out of the ordinary?"

"Besides Lindy, you mean?" Holly's voice was harsh.

Roberts nodded.

Holly glanced over at me again.

I said, "The door was unlocked. We walked in. The only thing that struck us as weird is that we couldn't find Lindy. Holly recognized her car, and so we knew she was here. But there was no sign of her." I hesitated. "I'd never been in the office before, but it looked like everything was in order to me. It didn't look like someone had ransacked the place, searching for something."

"Did you move the body?" asked Roberts.

Holly flinched at his reference to Lindy as a body.

I shook my head. "I only felt for a pulse once we found Lindy. We weren't expected to see her on the floor, of course." I swallowed. "But no, we didn't move her. And, when we left the building, I opened the door with a tissue. Of course, we didn't do that on the way inside."

Roberts nodded. "We're going to need to take your fingerprints so we can eliminate them."

Holly and I both nodded. But I knew the chances of finding the killer's fingerprints were pretty slim. It was a dental practice—there were going to be tons of fingerprints on every surface. Plus, the killer might have worn gloves.

Roberts said, "Tell me a little about Lindy. Did you know her well?"

Holly shook her head. "Not as well as I should have. She was my brother's girlfriend, of course—you knew that, right?"

Roberts bobbed his head to indicate he had.

Holly blew out a sigh. "Their relationship was still pretty new. Less than a year. I was surprised Frank had jumped right into a relationship like that. After all, I thought the divorce process had been rough on him."

"Your brother missed his ex-wife? June?"

Holly snorted. "No. No, I don't think he missed her at all. They were sort of an odd couple, I always thought. But the divorce itself was tough. June was trying to get more money and more assets, saying she deserved more. And it all seemed to drag on. I knew Frank just wanted it over and done with."

"You say they were going out for less than a year? Do you know when he started dating Lindy?" asked Roberts.

Holly considered this. "I don't *exactly* know, but I know it's been months. It wasn't like he was seeing Lindy at the same time he was married or anything. He was divorced when they started dating."

"Did that cause any issues at work?" asked Roberts. "Considering they were coworkers?"

Holly said, "Not as far as I know. I'm not sure Carl was thrilled about it. Of course, an office romance isn't great when things aren't going well, but Frank seemed really happy with Lindy. And she was devastated when Frank died." Holly's voice cracked a little at the end.

Roberts nodded. Then his gaze narrowed as a car entered the parking lot.

Chapter Seventeen

"That's Carl," said Holly.

Carl was looking around as if he was baffled by the chaos at his dental practice. Crime scene tape and emergency vehicles would surprise anybody. He was wearing scrubs and, seeing Holly and me speaking with the lieutenant, quickly came toward us.

"What's going on?" he barked before he'd even fully reached us.

"Maybe you'd like to have a seat, sir. Or speak with me over there." Roberts gestured across the parking lot."

Carl ignored this, his face flushed. "I asked what happened."

Roberts said, "I'm sorry, but Lindy Baker was found dead, just minutes ago."

"In the building?" Carl's voice rose.

"That's correct. Have you had any contact with Lindy recently?" asked Roberts.

Carl looked as if he was trying to process what Roberts had told him. "What?"

"Have you seen or spoken with Lindy recently?" asked Roberts patiently.

Carl nodded. "Well, sure I have. She's our receptionist. And bookkeeper, to boot. I spoke to her yesterday and asked when she'd be coming in to work. She took a little time off. It makes work complicated when she's not there. The phone rings off the hook all day long."

Holly was looking annoyed now, a red flush rising up her features. I had the feeling that Carl's casual mention of Lindy's absence was the source of her irritation. I got it—Carl wasn't acknowledging the fact that Lindy was grieving. He was solely focused on the business inconvenience of it all. The impression that I'd gotten of Carl so far was definitely not a favorable one. He seemed self-serving in every way; from wanting to sell the business right out from under his partner to thinking of himself in the situation he found himself in now.

This was reinforced when Carl said, "This is not good. Two mysterious deaths connected with my practice?" He shook his head. "I hope this won't scare off the buyer I've got."

Holly, unable to restrain herself anymore, said tartly, "I can't think of a worse thing that could happen, in the face of Lindy's death."

To his credit, Carl looked a little ashamed of himself.

Roberts might have been irritated by Carl, too, because he launched into a series of questions designed to make Carl very aware that he was certainly considered a suspect in these deaths. "Where were you this morning?"

Carl's eyes flashed. "Where do you think? I've been at home getting ready to come to work."

"Can anyone vouch for you?"

"No. I live by myself," said Carl. "I'm pretty sure I told you that the last time I spoke with you."

Roberts said, "I understand Lindy was considering leaving your practice. Were you aware of that?"

Carl frowned. "No, I was not. And I doubt very much that it's true. Lindy was far too responsible to have left the practice without giving notice. Besides, if she had no intention of working for me any longer, what was she doing here today?"

Roberts didn't answer that question. "Tell me more about the kind of person Lindy was."

Carl shrugged, seemed slightly flustered. "I don't know. She was very organized, which you'd expect from a receptionist and bookkeeper. She was a hard worker. The only issue I had with Lindy was the fact I thought having a workplace romance was inappropriate."

"You shared that opinion with her?" asked Roberts.

"Naturally. I was one of her employers. I thought it was in poor taste. And it wasn't my *opinion*—you can look anywhere online and see advice warning against those types of relationships. It's not good for the business."

I tightened my lips. Carl was laser-focused on the business. I couldn't really figure out why that was, considering he was so eager to sell it. He wasn't even very interested in continuing on as a dentist. I guessed he was just the kind of person who wanted control of a situation. And he'd been out of control for a while now.

"And personally? How was Lindy personally?" asked Roberts.

Carl looked at him as if he didn't completely understand the question. "Personally? I wasn't friends with Lindy. She was an employee. A good one."

Roberts seemed to try to keep his patience. "Yes, but you must have formed some sort of opinion about her."

Carl thought for a few moments. "Pleasant. Seemed to have a nice sense of humor. The patients liked her." He shrugged again.

Roberts said, "Okay. Thinking back on your relationship with Frank now."

"Relationship? Again, we had a work-related relationship," said Carl in a clipped tone.

"Right. But I hear it might have been strained. Your interest in selling the practice, for example. I understand it might have caused some tension between the two of you," said Roberts.

"Tension? No." Carl flushed. "I don't appreciate people saying that. We had a difference of opinion, that's all. People are entitled to have those. Besides, I had nothing to gain from either of these deaths. I resent the implication that I'm a suspect."

Roberts gave him a skeptical look. "It seems you might gain plenty from your dental partner's death. After all, you're now free to sell the practice without any issues. Perhaps Lindy realized you might be involved in Frank's death."

"I was working at the office during the time Frank died." Carl raised his chin in defiance.

Roberts' gaze was steely and unwavering. "That's interesting. Because I understand you were *not* in the office all morning."

Carl didn't say anything to this for a few moments. "It's a lie," he muttered. Then, frowning, "Do I need to get a lawyer?"

"Of course, if you feel you need representation. Do you need a lawyer?"

Carl shook his head angrily. "I don't. Look, I got along well with both Frank and Lindy."

I remembered Lindy's thoughts on Carl and how eager she was to leave the practice. I also remembered how startled Lindy had seemed when Carl had told Grayson and me he was in the office the morning of Frank's death. How she'd mentioned later that Carl had been in and out that day.

Carl continued, "No matter what you think of me, I'm not a stupid guy. And murdering Lindy, in my own office, would be stupid. It makes no sense."

Roberts said, "Then tell me what *does* make sense. Who do you think could be involved in these deaths?"

"Paul Hammond makes the most sense," said Carl eagerly. "He had the most to lose. You know that. If the police department looks the other way just because Paul is the mayor of Charleston, you're just as corrupt as he is."

"Tell me more about why you think Paul is guilty."

Carl spread his hands wide in an appealing gesture. "It's as plain as the nose on your face, Lieutenant. Paul had a stake in that development that Frank was digging around on. Paul probably pushed through the development without even disclosing he was getting a payoff. Then Frank found human remains on the site. He was an honest guy, so he let Paul know. But Paul couldn't afford to let that information leak out. He got rid of Frank to shut him up so that the development could proceed."

"And Lindy?"

Carl said impatiently, "It's just like you said. Lindy knew something. Maybe Frank told her what he'd found and why the site wouldn't be able to proceed." A car pulled into the parking lot and an elderly woman with a shock of white hair looked alarmed at all the emergency vehicles. Carl blew out a sigh. "When can I get my office back? Clearly, I've got patients coming over."

"Do you have a list of patients that are coming in today? Because I can promise you there's no way anybody will be seen."

Carl made an annoyed sound. "No, I don't have a list. Lindy had a list. The list is inside on a computer."

Roberts said, "I'm sorry to hear that. I'm sure your patients will understand. Maybe you can post a sign temporarily to inform them they'll need to reschedule."

Carl reddened. He didn't look exactly happy at this turn of events. He stalked off to speak with the elderly woman who was in her car with the window down, peering in Carl's direction.

Roberts said to us, "If you think of anything else you need to share with me, just let me know."

Holly and I nodded and got back into her car.

Chapter Eighteen

We both sat still for a few moments in the car after Holly started it up. A text came through on my phone, and I pulled it out of my pocket.

Is everything okay? It was Grayson.

I pecked out a quick explanation.

Oh no. Are you coming back to Holly's?

I glanced over at Holly, who seemed completely deflated. "Holly? Do you want me to drive?"

She nodded, hopping back out of the car as we changed places, and I got behind the wheel. "Is that Grayson?" she asked.

"Yeah. I just filled him in real quick. He wants to know if we're heading back to your place."

Holly shook her head slowly. "No. I think . . . no. Has Grayson eaten breakfast yet?"

I texted Grayson. "He says no."

"I'm starting to feel like I could have something. All I had this morning was coffee, and you didn't even have that. My stomach feels really off."

I said, "Are you sure you want food if you're not feeling well?"

"I think it's the kind of sick feeling you get when your body is dissatisfied with the fact you haven't eaten yet," said Holly, a wry smile on her features.

"Let's have a big breakfast, then. I'll text Grayson and ask him to meet us there."

Holly considered this. "Okay. We can go to a fancy place that has an elegant buffet and mimosas. Or we can go to a place that's a dive but has really divine comfort food."

"What are you feeling like?" I was hoping she'd say the dive because Grayson hadn't gotten that money yet, and he and I were always on a bit of a budget.

A smile widened Holly's mouth. "The dive. I want a sausage and egg biscuit. With maybe some hash browns on the side."

A few minutes later, we were in an orange vinyl booth with cups of steaming coffee in front of us and laminated menus in hand. We were lucky someone left the diner right as we arrived because the place was completely packed and now there were several parties waiting for a table.

Holly said, "Sausage and biscuit, hash browns, and a side of buttery grits. How about you two?"

Grayson was happily studying the menu. It was the kind of menu that had photos of the dishes, just in case you weren't sure what a biscuit looked like. He said slowly, "I'm trying to decide between a pancake plate or the three-egg breakfast."

"Mm! Tough one," said Holly. "I'm thinking you probably haven't had too many carbs lately. Feel like loading up?"

"I'm thinking I need reinforcements while I hear more about what happened this morning," said Grayson, looking serious. "May as well be carbs."

The server came by, took our orders, and refilled our already-pretty-full coffees. As she left to place the orders with the kitchen, Grayson said, "Okay. What happened?"

Holly looked at me. "Can you fill him in?"

I did. I told him about us running by the practice to deliver a photo and hoping to have the chance to see Carl. I told him how we got more alarmed as we couldn't find Lindy and where she was when we finally did. And I told him about Roberts coming.

Our food came as I was wrapping up. Grayson absently poured what looked like half a bottle of warm syrup on his pancakes as he absorbed what I said. "That's awful. Hey, I'm sorry I slept in. I should have been there with you." His face was grim. "What if the murderer had still been on the scene?"

Holly shivered. I said firmly, "Well, we were making so much racket calling for Lindy that he could easily have slipped out without confronting us. We weren't exactly sneaking up on anybody."

Holly said, "Don't feel bad about sleeping in. You needed the sleep. And Murphy loved all the attention you gave him yesterday. That was a huge help for me. I've been feeling bad that I haven't had time to really walk him."

Grayson gave her a small smile. We drank our coffee for a few moments. Then he said, "What happened after the cops came?"

Holly gave me a prompting look again. I said, "Roberts asked us some questions. He probably needed to eliminate us as suspects, I guess."

Holly nodded. "He wouldn't be doing his job if he didn't."

"Then Carl Hopkins came by. He wasn't thrilled about having a murder at the dental practice," I said.

Grayson raised an eyebrow. "The one he's trying to sell. No, I guess he wasn't. Even so, that probably came off pretty cold."

"Yeah, I think Roberts might have thought it sounded that way. He was still trying to get a lock on Carl's feelings about Frank, and the way Frank stood between him and selling the place. Carl seemed more concerned about what was going to happen when the patients came by and no one could get their dental work done."

Grayson said, "A legitimate concern, but again, it doesn't make him sound like the warmest person. Or that he cared much about Lindy."

Holly said, "It sounded like he thought of Lindy as just an employee. A capable one, for sure, but not someone who he cared anything about. It made me think, if she'd known something about Carl being involved in Frank's death, that he wouldn't have thought twice about getting rid of her."

"Is that what you think happened?" asked Grayson, looking somber.

Holly shrugged. "I don't know what to think. I felt like I was just starting to feel a little normal this morning, you know? That's really the ironic thing. I was processing the fact that Frank was gone and taking baby steps forward. Now this happened." She looked helplessly at us. "I want to find out who's behind this. Seriously. I know the cops are doing their jobs, but it's taking forever. What if more people die in the meantime?"

"You're wanting us to figure it out," I said. It wasn't a question. I could see Holly's intent on her face.

"I think we can do it. Especially since you've had some experience with this, Holly. People will talk more to us than they will to the cops. And we have a good angle for finding out information—it was my brother who died, after all. They'll understand if I want to talk about what happened. Or if I embark on a vendetta," she said dryly, picking up her sausage and egg biscuit to take a bite. After swallowing it down, she said, "Ann, can you give a rundown of all our suspects?"

"Sure. We've covered Carl already. And now Lindy is out of the picture, if she'd ever really been part of it," I said.

Grayson nodded. "I'm sure the cops probably thought of her as a major suspect for Frank's death. A girlfriend would be. But I couldn't picture it."

I said, "So we've got Warner the relic hunter, June the ex-wife, and Paul the best friend."

Holly said, "You know, I've always thought Paul was a great guy and a good friend to Frank. Frank always had a tendency to stay in his own head too much, but he'd be a different person with Paul. Paul was good for him, I'd always thought. And now? I just don't know what to think."

Grayson nodded soberly. "It doesn't look great, does it? It sounds like he might have been doing business on the shady side with that development."

"So, what are we thinking?" I asked. "We think the developer bribed Paul to help push the development approval through? Maybe offered him some sort of stake in the project? Or maybe Paul was in on the development all the way through and just didn't disclose it and recuse himself when it came up for a vote?"

Holly shrugged. "Either way, it stinks to high heaven. The whole thing really bugs me. Paul has plenty of money. He *came* from money. It's upsetting to me that he might be corrupt. Why would he need more money? Because of June and her crazy spending?" Her face darkened. "And what if he killed Frank because Frank stood in the way of him getting that money? And Paul was terrified of having his corruption uncovered?"

"At least the police know about Paul's involvement in whatever it was. It sure sounds like it might have been influence peddling, at the very least," I said. "So we agree he has a strong motive."

Holly and Grayson nodded.

"Then we have Warner," I said. "At first glance, he didn't seem to have as much motive as Paul. We know he was upset and probably jealous of Frank. Frank seemed to have a much more successful relic hunting operation than Warner did."

Grayson nodded. "I think a couple of things are key there. Warner sounded like he was frustrated with the status quo. He's putting everything into his relic hunting passion, but he wasn't as successful as Frank."

Holly shrugged. "Frank was a little older, and he had a lot more connections."

I said, "And Warner sounded pretty bitter about those connections."

"True," said Holly in a thoughtful tone.

Grayson added, "There's something else, too. The way Frank was murdered seemed impulsive, didn't it?"

"Totally," I said. "It's like someone noticed Frank's car outside the library, found him, maybe had an argument or a disagreement, and then pushed the bookcases over." I gave Holly an apologetic look at bringing up the way Frank had died.

But Holly, warming to the task of figuring out the most likely suspect, didn't even notice. "It doesn't seem planned, does it? It must have been spontaneous."

I nodded. "Unless somebody knew Frank's schedule that morning and waited for him."

Holly said, "I'm not even sure *Frank* knew his schedule. He kept things pretty flexible because people would call in with dental emergencies, and he'd fit them in." Her eyes widened. "But Lindy knew his schedule."

We looked at each other. I said slowly, "Which could be the reason Lindy was murdered. Someone could have called in, asked to speak with Frank, and then Lindy mentioned where he was. Later, she'd have wondered about that." A shiver went up my spine.

Holly shivered, too. "Okay. The next person up is June, the ex-wife. Of course, she's a natural suspect, even though their divorce wasn't exactly a nasty one."

Grayson said, "But why would she kill Frank? The divorce had already gone through; it wasn't like he was standing in the way of her getting married to Paul. Do you think she was asking for more financial support from Frank?"

Holly shook her head. "Why would she? Paul has a lot more money than Frank did. June was going to be set for life. But again, I think about the impulsive nature of the crime, like you were saying, Grayson. Maybe she was upset about something Frank had done a while back. Maybe she decided to give Frank a piece of her mind once she spotted his car in the parking lot. Then she got angry and shoved the bookcase down." Holly looked at us to see what we thought of this scenario.

I nodded. "It could have just been an irrational act. June is under a lot of stress and has been for a while. First, there was the unraveling of her relationship with Frank. Then there was new-relationship stress with Paul."

Grayson raised his eyebrows. "Is there such a thing as new relationship stress?"

"Oh, sure there is," said Holly. "You're trying to foster a new relationship and be on your best behavior. It's definitely a thing."

"Got it. Sorry for interrupting," said Grayson.

I smiled at him. "Anyway, then there was the divorce process, which could have been grueling. And then there was the wedding to plan. It's kind of a lot. So maybe she did just fly off the handle and do something she never would ordinarily think of doing."

Holly said, "And we've already talked a little about Carl. He really gave me a poor impression this morning. I got the feeling that he didn't care at all about what happened to Lindy or, by extension, Frank. The more I look at him, the more I think he can be cold-blooded enough to murder."

Grayson nodded. "He's definitely the kind of person who's used to getting what he wants. And Frank stood in his way."

I said, "Carl's high on the list, for sure."

We finished up our breakfast, still mulling over bits and pieces of the case. Holly said, "I think we should go see Warner."

"All of us?" I asked.

"Sure," said Holly. "I brought a couple of the relics from Frank's house. I made sure they were ones he had plenty of. We can run by his house on the premise of stopping by to deliver them to him. A nice gesture. I also told him I'd give him Frank's notebook. I'd like to find out a little more about Warner's friendship with Frank. Besides, it makes me feel better that I'm *doing* something."

"Do you think he'd be home now?" asked Grayson.

Holly shrugged. "No idea. It sounded like he had a pretty erratic schedule. We can give it a go. I just need to run by the house and grab the relics and notebook first."

We went by Holly's house, and Grayson and I let Murphy out while she grabbed a small tote bag. Then we set off, this time all in the same car.

Holly had looked up Warner's address online. He lived in an apartment building that looked like it had seen better days. We went up a few flights of dirty cement stairs to an apartment at the end of the hall. Holly knocked on the door.

After a couple of minutes with no response, Grayson leaned over and pounded on the door.

Chapter Nineteen

"Well, he definitely heard that," I said wryly.

I was glad to see a smile on Holly's face. She said to Grayson, "Investigative reporter technique?"

He gave a small bow and grinned.

Sure enough, the door opened, and a suspicious-looking Warner stood there. He was wearing raggedy gym shorts and an old tee-shirt. His hair was sticking up on his head and there were lines from the pillow or sheets on his face. He'd clearly just woken up.

When he realized who we were, his expression changed. "Oh," he said in a sleepy croak. "Hey guys."

"Sorry we just popped by like this," said Holly, not sounding very sorry at all, although she gave Warner a big smile. "We didn't mean to wake you up."

"I should already be up," said Warner, flushing pink. "I've overslept. I played video games pretty late last night." He paused, as if suddenly remembering his manners. "Want to come inside?"

A moment later, we were inside Warner's cluttered apartment. It might have been a sunny apartment had the heavy curtains not all been drawn. He looked around him, bemused, as if seeing his living room for the first time. Any flat surface was covered with stacks of books, notebooks, bags of various objects, or discarded meals.

"Sorry," he muttered. "Haven't had the chance to clean up here for a while."

He swiftly moved some things around and cleared several seats off. We sat down.

I thought Warner had a pretty good alibi for Lindy's death. He had clearly been knocked out cold when we arrived. Although I supposed he technically could have still been awake, murdered Lindy, and then turned in.

Grayson seemed to read my mind somehow. "I've got some buddies who are gamers. They stay up really late when they play."

Warner gave him an appreciative look. He'd obviously felt pretty sheepish about his game playing. "Yeah. It's easy to lose track of time. They're designed that way, you know? Pretty addictive. I was up all night. Actually, I just turned in about an hour ago."

Holly said, "Sorry. We really didn't mean to wake you up. We weren't even sure we'd catch you here." She reached into her tote bag. "Ann and I were at Frank's place, clearing things out. I found some relics there that I thought you might be interested in. And Frank's notebook that I told you I'd bring by."

Warner's entire countenance changed. He was suddenly genuinely awake; more than awake, he was alert.

Holly pulled out some buttons and a round object. She said apologetically, "I wasn't sure what this round thing was. It sort of looked like the top of a septic tank. But I figured if Frank had kept it, it had to be more important than that."

Warner nodded, eyes fixed on the round object as he reached for it. "It's a brass tampion. A cap for a military cannon."

Warner turned into a totally different person as he started talking about the cap and the buttons. He held them gingerly, lovingly. He spoke knowledgeably about the items. Then he said hesitantly, "What are you planning on doing with these things?"

Holly said, "These are for you to keep. It looked like Frank had others. I thought you might appreciate having them."

To my surprise, Warner actually got choked up. "Thank you," he said gruffly.

"I'm not sure what my plans are for the other things Frank has," Holly said. "My parents have tasked me with taking care of them. I'm leaning toward donating his finds to museums and universities instead of selling them to collectors."

Warner nodded. "Yeah. That's probably the right thing to do." He looked wistful for a few moments. "That's where I want to be with my relic hunting one day. Right now, I'm sort of living hand to mouth, so I have to sell whatever I find."

Holly said slowly, "I've heard that there are often tensions between relic hunters. Which totally makes sense. It's competitive, isn't it?"

Warner looked a bit wary. "I suppose it is."

"Someone Frank knew said the two of you had argued recently over his last dig," said Holly. She raised her hands as Warner's expression turned defensive. "I'm not saying you had anything to do with what happened to Frank. All I'm trying to do is figure out what happened to him. And separate the truth from fiction. I've heard plenty of gossip."

Warner didn't look as if he appreciated the prying. In fact, he looked as if he couldn't wait for us to leave so he could get back to sleep.

Warner said resentfully, "I wouldn't say that Frank and I argued. We might have had a difference of opinion. That's what happens sometimes, no matter what kind of business or hobby you have. If you feel passionate about something, you can get emotional about it."

Holly glanced over at me, wanting me to hop in. I cleared my throat. "We heard you might have been upset that Frank was using his connections to get some of the sites he had. Like the last one he was working on. We recently heard that a friend of his was involved with the site."

Warner looked a little more relaxed, less defensive. "Oh, you mean the mayor? Yep. Sure looks like Paul had a good motive to shut down Frank's digging."

"So you knew about that," I said.

Warner shrugged. "I spend a lot of time researching, and I'm good at it. I poked around online and then made a couple of phone calls. I found out that the mayor was the one who brought Frank onboard."

Holly quickly said, "But you don't think Frank would be part of anything shady, right?"

It was definitely a question. Holly wanted to believe her narrative that Frank wouldn't have gotten involved in any of the sketchy dealings the mayor might have been up to his neck in. But there must have been a part of her who wanted that clarified. There was a pleading note in her voice.

Warner said, "No, of course Frank wouldn't. That's why we were arguing before he died . . . if it *was* an argument. Like I said, it was more of a difference of opinion. Frank was sticking up for his friend and said Paul wouldn't do anything that wasn't on the up-and-up; that Frank had known Paul his whole life. I just reminded him that people can be funny when it comes to money."

He shook his head. "Frank didn't want to hear the truth. But I'm thinking Frank must have confronted Paul with what I'd told him. Then Paul had to shut him down."

Holly looked a little relieved that Warner agreed with her that Frank was ethical. "Okay."

Warner looked reminiscent. "Frank was definitely a rule follower, even with the unwritten rules of relic hunting. We had a young relic hunter who wanted to come along with Frank and me to a site. It was private property that the owner was allowing us to dig into. We had metal detectors out, and Frank and I had found a few cool things. The next thing we knew, this young guy had put something on his social media. The floodgates opened, and relic hunters from all over the place showed up. Their cars were trenching the guy's front yard."

Grayson said, "I bet the property owner was furious."

"Oh, he wasn't the only one. *Frank* was furious. Because discretion is one of those unwritten rules. Plus, Frank felt like the kid had violated the trust the property owner had placed in us. He gave him an earful."

Holly smiled. "I can see him doing that." Then she stopped smiling. "Thinking back to Frank's murder, have you spoken with the police yet?"

The wary look was back on his face. "Well, sure. You were there when I spoke to them at the library. I haven't talked to them since then, nor do I want to."

"The thing is, there's been another death."

Warner's eyebrows knit together. "What? You mean a death that's related to Frank's?"

She nodded. "Lindy Baker died this morning. She was murdered."

Warner sat back in his chair, looking stunned. He was either an excellent actor or else he was actually surprised. "What is going on?" he asked under his breath. Then he looked back at Holly. "How did you find out about this?"

Holly looked over at me. I could tell our awful discovery this morning was still weighing heavily on her. I said, "Holly and I ran by the dental office to give Lindy a photo that Holly found in Frank's house. She and I found Lindy."

Warner briefly closed his eyes. "Oh, man. This is so crazy."

"Did you know Lindy?" I asked.

He shook his head. "Nope. But Frank talked about her a lot. At first, it was like he was crushing on somebody at school or something. But then on, he acted like he was really in love. I was sure the two of them were going to get married." He sighed, stretching his hands out. "And now both of them are dead."

Holly wiped away a stray tear.

Grayson said, "So you're going to tell the cops that you weren't at the dental practice."

"Well, of course, that's what I'm going to tell them. Because I wasn't at the dental practice," said Warner, his voice rising to a squeak at the end. "You three could practically be my alibi, you know. You came over here, and I was obviously dead to the world. I was sleeping when this happened. Unless it happened in the middle of the night, which sounds unlikely. But if it happened at three in the morning, I was playing video games." He gave us a dignified look. "And if you'll forgive me, I'm going to return to bed now. I do have some things I need to take care of today, and I should get some sleep before I do."

We headed for the door. As we were walking out, Warner said stiffly, "Thank you for the relics and the notebook, Holly."

She gave him a small smile as we left.

We were heading for the stairs when a large bearded man stopped us. "You coming from Warner Andrews' place?" he demanded.

We nodded.

The man's bushy eyebrows knit together. "So he's there?"

Grayson said, "Yes. Although he was about to go to sleep."

The man snorted. "I don't care about his beauty sleep. I care about my rent. He's been trying to skip out on me."

I said slowly, "Well, he was there all night last night and this morning, too."

The bearded man put his beefy hands on his hips. "That's a lie. I set an alarm early this morning so I could catch him. When I got to his door, I looked out into the parking lot and saw him climbing into his beat-up car."

Chapter Twenty

We all froze, looking at each other. Holly said, "So he was gone this morning."

"Yep. Skipped out on me, like I said. He's not stupid, I guess."

Holly gritted her teeth, ran back to Warner's door, and pounded on it.

A weary voice came from inside. "I'll have the rent for you soon, Gus."

But Holly kept pounding.

He finally, cautiously, opened the door. Warner blinked in surprise when he saw Holly there. "Holly?"

"So you *weren't* at home sleeping when Lindy died. Your landlord just told us he saw you in the parking lot when he came over to collect your rent. Where were you?" she spat.

Warner looked worried. "I wasn't at the dental practice, Holly. Like I said, I didn't even know Lindy. Why would I? I just heard Frank talk about her."

"Where *were* you?"

The landlord folded his arms. "Yeah, I'd like to know that, too. Then I want my rent."

Warner sighed. "It was like I told you, Holly. I was playing video games. It's a good stress reliever, and I'd been feeling pretty stressed lately. It was really late when I realized what time it was. Maybe six-thirty or six-forty-five. I was getting ready to go to bed when I heard Gus's door slam and knew he was coming up to get his rent."

Grayson cocked a skeptical eyebrow. "You knew it was Gus's door? There are lots of residents here."

Warner shot him a look. "Yes, I knew it was him. He's a loud guy, okay? Nobody else slams their doors like that, especially that early in the morning. Also, he mutters to himself a lot. I knew it was him. He was downstairs, so I knew I just had a minute or two to get out of here. I was worried he was going to use his key."

Gus said, "Yeah, because it's not going to be your apartment anymore if I don't get that rent. It's my property."

"So all I did was run down the stairs, hop in my car, and get coffee until the coast was clear. I swear. I don't even know where the dental practice is," said Warner.

"It would be easy enough to find out online," said Holly, her eyes still suspicious slits.

Warner raised his hands. "Look, I didn't kill Lindy. And I didn't kill Frank."

The landlord now said, "What? What's going on? You're part of a murder investigation?"

"I'm *not*," said Warner. "I just knew one of the people. Not even all that well."

Holly looked like she was about to erupt.

Warner caught her eye and quickly said, "I'm sorry. I don't know anything about what happened to Frank and Lindy. I really don't. All I can tell you is that Frank complained about his ex-wife a lot. He thought she was being a real pain. Maybe she was the one who killed Frank."

I said, "But why would she kill Lindy?"

Warner eagerly said, "Because she was jealous. June still loved Frank and was jealous that he was interested in Lindy. I'm telling you, his ex-wife seemed like a real control freak to me. She kept calling him the last time I saw him. It was really bothering him. And there was plenty of bad blood between Frank and the mayor too, even if it might not have been obvious."

Holly said, "They were best friends."

"Sure they were. But best friends can get mad at each other, too. Paul is engaged to Frank's ex-wife. You can't tell me Frank wasn't mad about that on some level." Warner shrugged and looked angry. "Look, the only reason the cops are trying to make me out to be a suspect is because I'm not influential like everybody else. I'm poor. That makes me an easy target. I didn't kill anybody, and I'm ready to go back to sleep." He lifted his chin in the air.

"Okay," said Holly. "We'll leave you to it."

"No, we won't!" said a voice behind us.

I'd totally forgotten that Gus, the large, bearded landlord was there until he made his presence known again. "I want that rent, Warner. I'm evicting you if I don't get that money today. *Today.*"

"That's kind of unreasonable," muttered Warner. "I can't give you the money if I don't have it. And I don't have it."

"That's your problem! I'm running a business here. You said you were going to have the money last week. Then you said you'd have it yesterday. Now you're saying it's not ready today?"

Gus was pretty mad. I was glad I wasn't in Warner's shoes. I wondered how much the relics Holly brought to Warner were worth. Could they help pay his rent? Was he even thinking in that direction?

He apparently wasn't. He said defensively, "I'm on a dig right now. It's a really promising one, too. I looked at the Sanborn maps and the site's got tons of possibility."

Gus threw up his hands. "Maps? This is not what I want to hear. I told you last time; the whole reason I even rented this place to you, despite your poor credit record, is because of a *job*. A nine-to-five job. I had income verification. I didn't rent it to you because of maps. There's no promise in maps."

Warner said, "That's where you're wrong. There's lots of promise in maps."

"Here's an idea," said Gus. "Instead of staying up all night playing video games, get a night job. Work as a waiter, get a security guard gig . . . something. If I don't see that money today, I'm starting the eviction process."

With that, Gus turned and stomped away. Warner closed and locked the door after his very temporary reprieve. Holly, Grayson, and I slipped down the stairs to the car.

Chapter Twenty-One

"What a mess," Grayson said as we drove away.

Holly said, "I still don't know if I believe Warner or not. I mean, he totally lied to us about where he was this morning. He left his apartment."

"Yep. He sure didn't want to let us know," said Grayson. "Although it sounds like a pretty likely excuse. That he was running away from his landlord. That guy meant business."

"It's convenient, though," I said. "The fact that Warner was out during the time Lindy was murdered and then lied about it. He could have left his apartment for the very reason he said. Gus backed him up that he was on his way up to demand the rent. But then, while he was out avoiding Gus, he could have decided it was the perfect time to get rid of Lindy. She might have known too much."

"Well, we definitely learned how hard-up Warner is for cash," said Holly wryly. "It sounds like he's going to have to rob a bank today to make his rent payment."

"Those relics weren't worth enough to sell for rent, I'm guessing?" I asked.

Holly shrugged. "Who knows? I kind of doubt it. Maybe Warner is planning on borrowing money from somebody. Although Warner generally doesn't seem like the kind of person who has much of a plan. Gus had it totally right—how can you stay up all night playing video games when you know your rent is due? Why isn't he looking for some sort of job?"

I said, "It sounds like he's avoiding the situation. Like he doesn't have a solution, but thinking about it stresses him out, so he's focused on avoidance behavior. It isn't helpful, but it could be a coping mechanism for him."

"Well, I think he needs to cope by finding some kind of job. There's no other way for him to support his relic hunting." Holly sighed. "Sorry I'm so cranky. Grayson, Ann can tell you I'm not usually this irritable."

Grayson said, "You have lots to be upset about right now."

Holly said, "Yeah. I thought for a minute that we'd solved the case with Gus messing up Warner's alibi."

"We need to let the cops know about that. I have the feeling Warner might not be totally honest with the police," I said.

"Good idea. I'll call Roberts just as soon as we get back to the house."

And she did. She made the phone call while Grayson and I played ball with Murphy in the backyard. Murphy was wildly excited about the ball game and streaked back and forth across the yard until he got tired enough that he didn't return it, just parked himself under a bush to get out of the sun. Fitz gave himself a bath on the windowsill and watched us play with the dog.

Grayson said, "What do you think we should do today?"

I said, "I'll check with Holly to see if she has any firm plans. Or if she wants to head back over to Frank's house to clear out some more stuff."

Grayson nodded. "What if she doesn't have any plans? What do you feel like doing?"

"This is going to sound a little odd, but I think I want to go back to the library where Frank was found."

Grayson grinned at me. "You in a library? Definitely not the oddest thing I've ever heard, Ann."

I smiled back at him. "Fair enough. I was thinking maybe I could talk to the librarian, Meredith, about what Frank was looking at. Get her perspective on that. I was going to ask Holly if she wanted to come with us, too. Although she was looking at one point this morning like she really needed to get some rest."

We went inside with a happily exhausted Murphy, who was panting like a steam engine. Fitz watched him curiously, apparently not realizing that dogs could be so loud.

Holly smiled at us as we came in. I said, "I was thinking about going to the library. Maybe poke around and ask a few questions. Would you like to come along, or would you rather chill out here for a little while?"

Holly considered this for a moment. "I think it might be better if I let you tackle that yourself. I won't be a lot of help with research, although I bet Grayson would be. Investigative reporting, right?"

Grayson said modestly, "From time to time. There hasn't been too much to investigate in Whitby so far, but I did some before I got to Whitby."

Holly nodded. "I figured. I'll bow out of the library trip. But later today, I was thinking about going to speak with Paul. Want to come along?"

I nodded. Grayson said, "I might stick around at the house for that one, so he doesn't feel defensive with all three of us there."

"Good idea," said Holly. "Anyway, it would be nice to have some real ammunition against him in terms of that development. Right now, all we have is gossip. Maybe you can find the materials Frank was studying, and we can have some facts to ask Paul about."

We drove to the downtown library, which was apparently about to undergo some renovations and upgrades, according to signs we saw. It was much bigger than my usual stomping grounds in Whitby, of course, but still had that amazing library smell that I loved. Basically, I felt at home, even though it was an unfamiliar library. We asked a librarian for directions and she directed us to the South Carolina room on the second floor, which served as a reading room for The Charleston Archive. The archive apparently included pathfinders for property research and other areas of interest.

The room was quiet when we got there. There were tables for research and the walls were lined with glass display cases of valuable and interesting artifacts. There was a wall of file cabinets through a door in a restricted area, and bookshelves everywhere. I was glad to see that Meredith was working. She recognized us, too, and gave us a smile of greeting.

"How are things going?" she asked. "Do the police have any leads?"

"We don't really know. They haven't really been in touch to give any updates." I paused. "Grayson and I were curious about looking at what Frank was researching the morning he died. We thought it might help us understand a little more about what he was working on. I don't know if the police took the material with them or not, though."

The librarian shook her head. "They took a bunch of photographs, but they left the materials here. I know exactly what he was working on, since I re-shelved it after the police left."

"I'm guessing the materials here are closed-stack archives?" I asked.

The librarian nodded.

Grayson looked confused. "Closed-stack? Does that mean the public doesn't get access to them?"

I let the librarian answer. She said, "The public can't browse the collections—they must request specific materials. It's in place to protect the archive. But we didn't want to lock it up entirely, of course. We wanted everything to be accessible, but protected and preserved."

"What types of materials are in the archive?" asked Grayson curiously.

I could tell the librarian loved talking about the archive. Her enthusiasm was contagious as she warmed to her subject, even though Grayson and I lived hours away in a different state.

"The Charleston Archive focuses on public history. We're especially interested in archiving information about the history of Charleston in all different areas, from the cultural to the political. We have extensive genealogical information available on microfilm. We also house police and fire records dating back to the mid-1800s, historic photos, ephemera from the 1800s—it's a large collection."

Grayson asked, "What kinds of patrons do you have coming in here? Are they mostly genealogists?"

"We get tons of genealogists, for sure. But we also get lots of engineers, contractors, and architects."

I said, "They're wanting to know more about the property, I'm guessing? See if there might be any roadblocks to construction?"

"Sure. But a lot of them just want to renovate and then be able to talk about the history of the property—preserve it as a draw. Aside from them, we also see a lot of historians and academics." She smiled at me. "And I suppose I can add librarians to the list now."

I smiled back at her.

We chatted about the materials and some of the librarian's favorite items in the collection. Then she pulled out some records and pulled up the Sanborn maps on one of the library computers. The maps were fascinating, but I wasn't totally sure what I was looking at.

Grayson wasn't, either. "Is there a key for the maps? I'm not sure what the different colors indicate."

The librarian showed us the key. "Basically, they're showing the building materials for the structure. Pink is brick and tile, yellow is wooden. You can see the height of the buildings, how many stories each had, and the use of the structure; *d* is for dwelling, for instance. You can also see stores, hotels, churches, warehouses, and other buildings listed."

"I'm thinking one thing we might look for is the location of any burial grounds or cemeteries," I said. "Would those be listed on the maps?"

"Sometimes they are. But often, they're not. From the 1670s to the 1920s, many thousands of people were buried in unmarked graves in the city."

Grayson and I glanced at each other.

The librarian said casually, "I actually noticed what your friend was looking at on the computer. I'm a strict believer in patron privacy, but under the circumstances, I'm imagining he would want the information released."

She leaned forward and scrolled to a particular spot on the maps. "It was a large dwelling. Large enough to have its own family burial ground."

I said, "I've understood, just through conversations with various people, that construction would halt on a development if human remains were located on the site."

The librarian nodded. "That's correct."

"What would happen," I asked, "if someone covered up the discovery in order to let construction of the development proceed?"

"It's unlawful," said the librarian. "I can pull up the law for you, if you'd like."

"That would be great."

Grayson and I huddled over the computer as the librarian left to look up the information. Grayson said, "If Paul killed Frank because he was worried Frank was going to be a whistle-blower, wouldn't he have made sure the research material in front of Frank wasn't pointed to the project he was working on?"

"I was wondering that, too. But then, I guess he might have gotten scared away before he could close the window on the computer. That bookshelf coming down would have made a terrific racket, and the staff isn't far away since the area is closed-stack. Or maybe Paul couldn't even really tell what Frank was looking at. These are hand-drawn maps we're talking about."

Grayson said slowly, "We were originally thinking, or at least I was, that an argument must have ensued between Frank and his killer. Then the murderer impulsively shoved the bookcase over on him. But, being here in this room, that seems pretty unlikely."

It did. It was quiet in the room right then, but it felt as if somebody could come in at any time. Plus, the staff, even if they were pulling materials for patrons, weren't far away. It felt very risky.

"Whoever killed Frank must have been desperate," I said.

The librarian joined us again with her laptop. "Here we go," she said. "The law regarding penalties for damaging graves, gravestones, or other cemetery features."

Grayson and I read it quietly. Then I said, "So it's against the law to damage human remains."

Grayson added, "Or to remove them or a portion of them."

"Not only that," I said, "but it's a felony."

The librarian summed up, "A person could serve as many as ten years. And they'd be fined five-thousand dollars."

We were quiet for a few moments. I said, "That would be a real game-changer for someone's life."

The librarian nodded. Another patron approached her. "Let me know if I can find anything else for you."

After she'd walked away, Grayson said, "Paul had a lot to lose."

"And not just income. He has his political life and his reputation to consider. If a backroom deal had come to light, all of that would have been in peril," I said.

We looked at the computer again and the large dwelling where the development had apparently been intended.

"Let's look up the address and see what kind of information we can find," I said.

When looking up the address, I found a story about an apartment building that was going up on the site. The construction was due to start in a month.

"Nothing mentions the mayor's involvement," said Grayson after skimming the article.

"No. I'm guessing he's either a silent partner or else he's receiving money under the table for allowing the project to be approved."

Grayson said slowly, "We could speak with the developer's office. Ask a few questions."

Chapter Twenty-Two

I raised an eyebrow. "Do you think they'd speak with us?"

"I'll tell them I'm a journalist. Usually, developers like to get press."

"Unless they're doing something underhanded," I said.

"Right. But I'm guessing that there's just one person at the top who knows about any sort of payoff. Whoever does their marketing might be happy to talk about the development. Free publicity."

I nodded. "Makes sense."

Grayson stood up. "Let's head over there."

"What? I thought you were just going to call them on the phone."

Grayson grinned at my discomfort. He knew I was always a little awkward when he went into reporter mode. "I think we might find out more in person. We can charm them."

I snorted. "I'll just stand back and let you charm them."

Which is what I did. We located the management office for the developer, let the librarian know we were leaving, and headed to Grayson's car. A few minutes later, we were walking into a sleek, modern building. A man at the reception desk let a public relations representative named Wendy know we were there, and she came out shortly and directed us to her office.

Wendy was extremely professional. And, as Grayson had anticipated, she was eager to discuss the impending development. She presented a model of the apartment complex, which Grayson duly took pictures of. Wendy gave a polished spiel about the planned amenities at the building, the parking, and the number of units.

Grayson asked if there had been any trouble with getting the development approved. Wendy smoothly replied that approval had been no trouble at all.

Grayson gave Wendy one of his most winning smiles. "I understood your team invited relic hunters to come out to the site."

Wendy returned the smile, showing a set of very white teeth. "We do like to partner with local relic hunters in order to preserve any finds on our properties. The relic hunters we use are always very professional and treat their dig like a potential archaeological site."

"And were there any finds on the property?" Grayson quirked an eyebrow.

A polite smile in return. "Unfortunately not. I say unfortunately, because it's often fun for the development team when the relic hunters make discoveries. Sometimes they'll find a horse's tack or buttons. It's always interesting." She paused and lowered her voice as if someone might listen outside the door. "Although this time, I half expected there would be a major discovery."

"Why do you say that?" I asked.

Wendy said, "I suppose it must have been an appealing site. There was some interest from another relic hunter, although we'd already contacted one."

"And was anything discovered?" I asked.

Wendy shook her head. "No, despite the fact that it apparently seemed so promising. The way the other relic hunter was acting, I thought it was going to pan out to have lots of artifacts." She shrugged. "I guess you really can't tell."

"The way the other relic hunter was acting?" asked Grayson with a smile.

"Oh, he was furious. He wanted to explore the site, too. In fact, he asked for permission. But we'd already made arrangements with the one." She shrugged again. "The other guy wasn't too pleased about that."

"What did he look like?" I asked.

Wendy took the question in stride, perhaps used to journalists and their whims. "He was young, thin. Sort of unkempt, actually."

Grayson and I glanced at each other. Warner.

"And when did this altercation happen?" I asked.

It had been the day before Frank died.

Grayson asked a few more softball questions about the development and continued jotting down notes as Wendy waxed poetic about it. Then we finally took our leave.

"Warner wasn't happy about Frank getting the site," said Grayson grimly.

"Sounds that way. We'd heard he thought Frank was getting better sites because of his networking, but having an argument with Frank the day before Frank died is something else entirely."

We returned to Holly's house and filled her in about what we'd learned in the library and with the developer. She asked a few questions, then rubbed her head. "How is this all getting even more complicated as we go along?" Then she gave us a rueful look. "Sorry. You've both done a great job uncovering information. I guess it just muddies the waters a little."

The doorbell rang, and Murphy exploded into barking. Fitz moved behind a chair, but watched with interest as Holly moved to the door. After looking through the peephole, she turned and raised her eyebrows at us before opening the door to Paul Hammond.

The mayor of Charleston was standing there in a suit and tie, looking as if he was about to attend an important meeting or event. He again looked as if he hadn't slept at all, and hadn't for quite some time. There were dark circles under his eyes and stress lined his handsome features.

Holly said, "Paul. Won't you come in?"

He stepped inside and then noticed Grayson and me for the first time. He winced. "Sorry. I forgot you still had company."

"Oh, Ann and Grayson aren't really company. In fact, they've been so helpful this week that I'm thinking of making them honorary members of the family."

We settled in Holly's comfortable living room. Murphy had, thankfully, stopped barking and now seemed to embark on a campaign to get as much of his light-colored fur on Paul's dark suit as possible. It appeared to be a successful enterprise, although Paul took no notice.

Paul jumped right into the reason for his visit. "I heard about Lindy's death," he said somberly. "I can't believe there's been another murder."

Holly nodded. "I know. I feel the same way."

I could tell Holly was trying hard to be polite. She seemed, understandably, very reserved. After all, she'd been planning on meeting up with Paul later that day to question him more about his involvement with the development and Frank's discovery.

She must have been reading my mind because she said, "I was actually planning on seeing you today. I felt like I needed to talk some things over with you. This whole thing with Lindy has made the situation even worse. Have you heard from the police or the D.A. whether there have been any developments in the case?"

Paul shook his head. "Sorry, but no. That's not information I would ordinarily be privy to, either."

"But the police did question you about Lindy, I'm guessing. I thought maybe you might have learned about any developments then." Holly's voice was harsh.

Paul didn't seem to notice that Holly was angry. Or, if he did, he must have attributed it to the stress she was under. "They didn't divulge anything."

"But they asked you questions," pushed Holly.

"Yes. They wanted to know where I was this morning."

We waited, but Paul apparently didn't feel like being forthcoming.

"And where were you?" I asked, with a smile tempering the words.

Paul said, "I had a late start this morning. I haven't been sleeping well since Frank's death. I was still at the house when Lindy died."

"With June?" I asked. I wasn't sure if June had already moved in with Paul or if they were waiting until later.

Paul hesitated. "As much as I'd like to give myself an alibi, June was still at her place. She's been trying to pack and downsize some of her things before the wedding."

Holly gave me a prompting look. She apparently thought that I was doing a good job getting information from Paul. I said, "How well did you know Lindy?"

"I didn't know Lindy at all. I'd never met her."

I said, "I see. That's funny, because I thought you and Frank were best friends. It seems like he should have introduced you and Lindy."

"Sure, we're best friends. I mean, were. But we were also both really busy people. If I hadn't been so busy with work and with wedding planning, I'd have had Lindy and Frank over for a meal and gotten to know her. It just didn't happen that way. And now, it feels like life is even busier. June and I have been dashing around trying to get June moved in at my place. Plus, the wedding planning. There's been a lot going on at work, too. I haven't had the chance to even *see* June that much. And we're engaged. That's not the way it's supposed to be."

Holly had her arms wrapped around herself as if she were cold. Or as if she felt defensive, which was totally understandable.

Paul noticed, too. He said slowly, "I'm sorry, Holly. This is just one more awful thing to happen to you in the space of a week. What can I do to help you out?"

Holly gave him a small smile. "I don't know if there's anything you can do, although I appreciate the thought. I just want this to be over. I don't want anyone else to lose their life, and I want the police to figure out who's behind all this." She looked Paul in the eyes. "Any ideas who might be involved?"

Paul blew out a sigh, looking uncomfortable. "Of course, I don't *know* anything. And I would feel strange implicating anyone."

He looked more than uncomfortable. He looked almost ill. Although the murders were weighing heavily on Holly, it looked as though they'd kept Paul up at night. And, perhaps, from eating. He looked lighter than he had since I'd recently seen him, and he hadn't needed to lose a single pound.

Paul slowly continued. "Like I said last time, I keep thinking that Frank's dental partner has to be involved. Especially now that a second murder has taken place—and it's at the practice. From what I understand, Lindy's death is connected to Frank's. Maybe Lindy put two-and-two together, realized Carl was the one who'd murdered Frank, and confronted Carl about it. Everything seems centered on that dental practice."

"Just so Carl could sell out and move out of state?" asked Grayson.

Paul looked defensive. "If you think about it, the need to be autonomous is a big motivator. Carl was probably getting increasingly frustrated over his inability to convince Frank that he needed to sell."

Holly paused and then asked, "I hate to ask this, but are the police treating you as a suspect, Paul?"

Paul stiffened, his gaze chilly. "I wouldn't say that. I'm sure they're handing everything according to protocol. Anyone who was close to Frank would be someone the police would want to speak with. I'm sure they did the same for you, Holly."

Holly said wryly, "Yes. But then, I have my handy-dandy alibis right here." She gestured to us.

Paul continued, "There's no reason for the police to be interested in me. Frank and I were friends—the best of friends. I loved Frank like a brother. You know I did."

Grayson said, "Has the press made the connection yet? Between you and Frank?"

Paul shook his head. "There's no reason for them to. Of course, I have political adversaries who would want nothing more than to bring me down. They're going to be fanning the flames of this story until it's a wildfire."

"That's got to be exhausting," I said. "Thinking about all the trouble that could happen if the story were to get out."

Paul looked even more haggard than before as he considered it. "Maybe I should just leave politics behind. It's more of a headache than I thought it would be."

Holly was quiet for a few moments. Then she said, "Look, Paul, I can't sit on this any longer. You've been friends with my family for a long time. I've always thought of you as a second big brother."

Paul gave her a shaky smile.

"But I've heard some things that have really disturbed me. I hate to think you might be involved in anything that's underhanded, because that's not who I believe you are."

Paul swallowed, staring straight at Holly, as if unsure he wanted to hear what she was about to say next.

"I hear Frank was working on a dig for you. For a site that's going to be an apartment complex. That you might have received a payout for clearing the way for it to go through." Holly paused.

Paul's face was expressionless, just with that same exhaustion.

Holly took a deep breath. "Then Frank found something. I don't think it was more belt buckles or ammunition. I think this time he must have found something guaranteed to stop construction. Human remains."

Paul swallowed. "Holly, I know what you're thinking. But you're wrong."

"Am I? Because I really want to believe I'm wrong. I care about you, Paul. And I hate myself for even thinking that you could murder my brother. Was that what happened? Were you desperate to make sure the apartment complex proceeded on schedule? I discovered evidence that Frank had found human remains at that site. Did you get rid of Frank so he wouldn't report his findings?"

Paul gave a short, shaky, humorless laugh. "Because he *would* have reported them. You know that."

"You bet I know it. I told Ann and Grayson the same thing. Frank was a highly ethical person. He wouldn't turn his head and look the other way."

Paul nodded, looking at the floor. "No. And he didn't." He paused. "Frank did make a discovery of human remains. He came right to me about them. And, to my everlasting shame, I wasn't immediately receptive to hearing about this roadblock."

"Because you were financially invested in the project coming to fruition," I said.

Paul nodded, glancing up at me for a minute. "Yes. I needed some time to come around to the fact that I was going to lose out on a good deal of income."

Holly threw up her hands. "Paul. You have *plenty* of money. Money has never been an issue for you. You had money when you were a kid, even."

Paul turned his wan face her way. "You know how it is, Holly. When you have money, you need more money. It's almost like an addiction."

Holly pressed her lips together as if not wanting to say what she thought about the love of money being an addiction.

Paul rubbed his face, looking exhausted. "Look. I didn't react well. I pushed back at Frank. Those bones could easily have been from the 1700s. It wasn't like a recent resting place. It would have been easy to overlook . . . for anybody but Frank."

I said, "Grayson and I were over at the developer's office today. They didn't say anything about the project being on hold or experiencing any sort of delay. You must not have informed them yet."

"I'm going to," said Paul quickly. "It's just been very busy lately. Plus, I haven't been feeling well, which is probably because I haven't been sleeping. But I'm definitely speaking with them." He looked down at the floor again. "The last time I spoke with Frank, he just looked so disappointed in me. Like he didn't quite know who I was. He's my conscience in this." He looked back at us. "And I promise you, I didn't lay a finger on Frank. I would never have hurt him."

"So you're doing something underhanded, Paul?" Holly gave him a deeply disappointed look that made him flush.

"It wasn't exactly underhanded. But it wasn't exactly something I'm proud of. Not something I'd want the press to find out." He paused, looking at us. "But I don't want you to think that I'm going to emerge from this unscathed. As soon as my term is over, I'm resigning from my position as mayor."

There was a voice from behind us. "What? You can't do that, Paul. You're good for this city."

Chapter Twenty-Three

We turned around to see June standing there.

"Sorry," said June, sounding unrepentant. "I saw Paul's car here and heard your voices. I tapped at the door, but no one heard me."

I thought it must have been a very light tapping if June had knocked at all. It wasn't as if anyone was raising their voices. It seemed to me as if June had just walked in.

Paul immediately stood up, his face wary. "Hi, June. I should head out—I have a meeting shortly. I didn't mean to spend so much time over here."

I noticed there wasn't much warmth between Paul and June, especially as a newly engaged couple. Or, maybe, the warmth was just on June's side. She reached out to give Paul a hug, and it seemed as if he ducked away from it a little. He brushed his lips lightly against her cheek. I had the feeling he was trying to escape having a conversation about his political future with June. I could definitely see why. June was clearly pro-politics.

"Okay," said June. "We'll talk about this decision to leave politics later."

Paul sighed. "There's nothing to talk about. The decision is mine and mine alone."

June clearly pictured herself as the mayor's wife. Her eyes narrowed at Paul's words. "Like I said, we'll talk later."

Paul muttered a goodbye to us and quickly left.

June said, "Goodness! What happened over here to make Paul say something like that? Everybody I talk to says how great he's been for the city of Charleston. He cares so much about the people who live here. Plus, he's the kind of guy who can make things happen. He's able to push legislation through and influence the right people. He can't give up now, just because he's had a rough week."

Holly sounded irritated, probably because she was still upset by Paul's ethical lapse. "Like Paul said, it's really his decision. No one else's."

"But what will he *do* if he's not in politics? Play golf all day? Sit around the house?" This was apparently anathema to June.

Holly was now getting even more irritated than she already was. "He's having a tough day, June. In fact, we all are. You might not have heard the news, but Lindy Baker is dead."

"Who?" June peered at Holly.

"Lindy Baker. You know her. The bookkeeper and receptionist for Frank's dental practice. We were just talking about her the other day. And she was dating Frank." The last was definitely a dig at June. But I could understand her saying it.

"Ohh." June paused. "Okay. That's right. I kept thinking her name was Mindy or something. I had no idea that she's dead. That happened today? That's so weird."

Holly, who was apparently done, said sharply, "The thing that's weird about it is there's someone running around murdering people. So you haven't heard from the police yet?"

June stared at her, frowning. "No. Why would the police want to talk to me?"

Holly looked at me as if she didn't trust herself to answer politely.

I said, "It's because usually police want to speak with people a second time after another related incident."

June shrugged. "I'm not even sure why they wanted to speak with me the first time. It's not as if I'd been spending a lot of time with Frank. I sure don't know Lindy, so they'll be wasting their time and resources if they come to speak with me about her death. I just talked to her when I had to call Frank's office." She paused, as if remembering she should show some sort of remorse over the death of the young woman. "Of course, I'm very sorry to hear about her passing. What a terrible thing."

"Have you been out and about this morning?" Holly asked. "Because the police might have tried to come over and you weren't there."

She gave Holly a sharp look, as if realizing Holly was fishing for an alibi. "Oh, I was packing up stuff most of the time. But then I had to drive to Goodwill and drop a lot of things off. You know the drill."

Holly said, "Since you're so busy, you must have had an important reason to stop by here."

It was a prompting sort of statement, but it seemed to go over June's head.

"An important reason?" she asked.

Holly gritted her teeth. "I was wondering why you came by my house. Since you have so much going on."

"Oh, it's because I saw Paul's car here. The both of us have been so busy and occupied that we've hardly had a moment together."

Holly said, "Got it. Paul said something like that, too."

Grayson said, "You saw Paul at the engagement dinner, of course. You were both there."

June shrugged, looking away. "You know how those kinds of events are. I didn't actually get to spend much time with Paul that night. We were both catching up with people." She glanced at me, and I wondered if she could read my mind. She'd seemed to enjoy herself at her party, Paul or no Paul. June clarified, "I mean, it was *fun* to catch up with people. I just haven't had much of a chance to see Paul. When I saw his car, I thought I'd pop by. Too bad he was on his way out."

"What did you think of Lindy?" asked Holly, still pushing for more.

June looked a little irritated. "Like I said, I didn't really know Lindy. But I liked the *idea* of Lindy, if you know what I mean. I liked the fact that Frank was seeing someone. That was one of the worst things about breaking up with Frank—the fact that I knew he was going to be alone."

June made it sound like it was just a minor breakup instead of a divorce. But then, maybe that's how she and Frank both looked at it—as something that wasn't a big deal. Considering the fact that it seemed to have been amenable and didn't involve custody of children, that might have been the case.

June continued, "I always felt like Frank spent too much time with his dusty old maps, history, and relics."

Holly was apparently still feeling combative. And, since it concerned her murdered brother, a bit defensive. "That's the way he always was. It was something he cared about and loved doing. It sounds like it was something you didn't really understand about him."

"Oh, I know. I guess I just wished he'd pay as much attention to me as he did to his relics." June's mouth twisted a little. "Anyway, the point is that I'm glad he was dating someone."

Holly said, "That wasn't what you said about Lindy earlier. You seemed down on the relationship."

"Well, the more I think about it, the more I'm glad that Frank was with someone, especially since he didn't have much time left. But I had reservations, sure. I was still looking out for Frank, you know. I still wanted what was best for him."

"And Lindy wasn't what was best for him?" Grayson asked. The way he said it was gently curious—apparently a tone that June responded well to.

She gave him a smile. "Probably not. But she worked out for the short term. I didn't think Lindy would ultimately make him happy, though. She didn't seem much of a match for him intellectually."

I'd been thinking the same thing, but in regard to June. June seemed too shallow and not academic enough to have been a good partner for Frank. The more I spent time with her, the more I thought the end of their marriage made sense. Plus, June should have expected what life with Frank would have been like. His relic hunting was far from a secret, and he'd been getting regular acclaim for it within his community.

"Plus," added June, "everyone knows you're not supposed to date someone at work. Still, I'm glad he was with someone at the end. And now, I've recalibrated and think I know who's responsible for all this. It's got to be Carl. I've been talking with Paul about it, and he seems absolutely positive that Carl's the one who killed Frank. And Lindy now, too, I guess."

"I thought you hadn't been speaking with Paul lately," Holly said, eyes narrowing.

June shot her a look. "We've been texting, though. Paul checks in with me. And he shares his thoughts."

Was that really true, though? It seemed like Paul couldn't wait to get away from June when she unexpectedly showed up. But I figured June might be different when she wasn't as keyed up as she was now. She seemed almost hyper, full of excess energy. Stress, like wedding planning stress, might cause someone to be that way.

"Why do you think it could be Carl?" asked Grayson, still in that innocuous, curious tone.

He was rewarded with another smile from June. "Oh, mainly because he was so invested in selling that practice. Frank could be super-stubborn, you know. Once he decided something, you couldn't change it. There was no way he was going to be convinced otherwise. I think Carl kept pushing him and pushing him and Frank kept pushing back. Then Carl followed him to the library, maybe thinking he would catch him off-guard. I think he just got fed-up with Frank and killed him. I don't think it was planned at all. I simply can't picture Carl lurking around a library, looking for a good opportunity to murder someone. It must have been totally spontaneous."

I said, "So you and Paul are convinced it's Carl."

June held up a hand. "Well, hold your horses. I'm not *totally* convinced that it's Carl. I mean, Paul made a great case for it. I think it *could* be Carl. But it could also be that weird research guy that Frank hung out with sometimes. Wallace? Winston?"

"Warner," we all chorused.

"Yes, that one. I always felt like that guy was far too caught up in the whole relic hunting thing. Frank was too, like I was saying earlier. But I honestly think Warner was worse."

Holly got fired up again. "Frank's hobby was fine. He wasn't hurting anybody, and he was contributing to museums and other groups. Educating others about history and how it's still alive. He didn't deserve what happened to him."

June raised a well-groomed eyebrow. "And I didn't say he did. I'm sorry if you took offense. I was just commenting that Frank was avid in his pursuit. But he wasn't as avid or as hungry as that Warner guy is. Warner was also really competitive. I wouldn't have put it past him to have gotten rid of Frank just so Warner could get better sites. Because the way it stood, Frank was getting the cream of the crop."

"And that was bothering Warner," said Grayson.

"Sure. I know that because he'd call Frank on the phone and both threaten him and plead with him to include him at different sites. Frank was so high profile that he was getting offers to do relic hunting all the time—he could honestly pick and choose between the offers. He'd sometimes give Warner the ones that seemed less interesting or less promising or whatever."

We waited, wanting to hear if June had anything else to add. She shrugged. "And that's all I know. Now, I really should head on out. Maybe Paul's meeting is wrapping up and he and I can spend some time together."

Holly asked, "Is Paul doing okay? He hasn't really seemed well lately."

June stiffened. "Of course he's doing well. He couldn't be happier. He's engaged to be married."

Her tone suggested that dire things would happen to Paul if he *weren't* extremely happy. I wondered if she'd even noticed he was down. Maybe she'd been so busy that she just hadn't seen it.

"Okay," said Holly shortly.

June frowned. "What makes you think he's not doing well?"

"It just looks like he hasn't been sleeping well. That he has a lot on his mind."

"Well, duh," said June with a short laugh. "He has a lot on his mind. Not only has his friend died, but he's about to get married. There's a lot going on."

"And he's thinking about a job change," added Grayson.

He was decidedly not rewarded with a smile this time.

June said decisively, "Paul will not be thinking about a job change. He's incredibly valuable to the city of Charleston. Plus, public service is in his bones. In his DNA! Everyone says that. He could even use the job as a springboard to bigger things—help out on a larger level. Make a real difference."

I said, "You mean by running for a bigger office? State house or senate?"

June threw up her hands. "Why even limit it? He could run for US house or senate. The point is that the sky is the limit and the last thing Paul needs to do is limit himself. If he *is* going through a rough patch, which I *don't* accept, it's just because he's a little rundown. Some sleep, some healthy food, and exercise are just what he needs. Plus, time with me."

"He sure seemed eager to get away from you earlier," muttered Holly.

June's gaze was icy in return. "He had a meeting."

Then June switched back to whatever her mental to-do list was to get Paul back to his usual self. Sure enough, she said, "After Paul is finished with whatever this meeting is, he and I can go to the gym. We haven't done that for a while. Then I can cook him a healthy meal. After that, he should be able to get a good night's sleep with no trouble." June glanced at her watch. "I should get going so that I can head to the store and pick up a few things for supper."

She said goodbye distractedly and then quickly took her leave.

Chapter Twenty-Four

Holly just shook her head. "June could totally be behind this. She doesn't have an alibi for either death. And she's just so cold-hearted and unfeeling sometimes. I don't know how she couldn't see how bad-off Paul is. I mean, he is her fiancé. It should be easy enough for her to recognize that he's not doing well right now."

Grayson said, "At least she seems like she has some idea of it now. And, obviously, a plan. The plan was a good one, too."

I said, "True. But it sure didn't look like Paul was eager to spend time with June. He couldn't leave fast enough when she arrived. Maybe time spent with June will make him worse instead of better."

Holly arched her eyebrows. "That's something he needs to realize before he gets married. There won't be a lot of room for escape once they tie the knot. And it sounds as if June already has his life planned out."

Grayson grinned. "Yeah. She's apparently going to push Paul until he ends up in the White House."

Holly said, "It was interesting that June realized Warner made for a good suspect. I've gotten the impression recently that June isn't the most observant person, but she did pick up on Warner." She pulled her phone out of her pocket. "I want to talk to that guy again." She looked in her contact list and then called a number. Apparently, the phone was ringing a lot on the other end. She made a face. "Guess I'll leave a message."

After the beep, Holly said sternly, "Hi Warner. It's Holly. Give me a call when you get this—I really need to speak with you." She put the phone down and said, "Okay, now I want to take a break from all this; at least until Warner calls me back. What are y'all in the mood to do?"

Grayson and I looked at each other.

"Honestly," said Grayson, "I'm in the mood to chill out for a while. Maybe curl up with Murphy or Fitz and read my book. How about you, Ann?"

"That sounds perfect right now. I need to recalibrate," I said.

"What are you reading, Ann?" asked Holly.

"I was trying to get into the Charleston mindset, so I picked up *The House on Tradd Street* by Karen White."

Holly nodded approvingly. "Oh, that's a good one. And we were on Tradd Street just the other day! A nice touch of mystery, great local background, and a ghost to boot."

So quiet time it was. I curled up with Fitz on Holly's sofa, and Murphy followed Grayson upstairs to hang out with him. Holly put in earbuds and listened to music while she did some housework.

After a couple of hours went by, Grayson came back downstairs, looking rueful. "I had every intention of reading my book, but somehow, I fell asleep."

Holly and I grinned at him. I said, "I must have had the more interesting book."

Holly said, "Hey, I understand falling asleep. I was just thinking that I needed to get out of the house and run a couple of errands. Do either of you need anything at the store?"

"If you don't mind, Holly, I wouldn't mind coming with you. I've got a few things I should pick up," said Grayson.

"Sounds good. How about you, Ann?"

I shook my head. "I'm good here. I guess I'll hold down the fort while you're gone."

Ten minutes later, Grayson and Holly headed out to Grayson's car. Grayson had a bigger vehicle, and Holly had mentioned getting some extra pavers and bags of fertilizer at the hardware store. "See you later," I said as they walked out the door.

It was probably five minutes later when there was a knock on the door. I figured Holly or Grayson had forgotten their wallet and came back to collect it.

But when I opened the door, I saw June standing there.

If I was surprised to see June, she was downright startled to see me. She drew back a little. "Where's Holly? I saw her car here."

"Gone to run an errand," I said briefly.

June looked confused. "Wait. You two are staying here at the house with Holly? I thought you were in an Airbnb and just visiting her from there."

"Holly was kind enough to invite us to stay at the house."

June seemed ill at ease. "I should go."

I shrugged. "But you came here for a reason, didn't you? You wanted to see Holly. I'm happy to pass a message to her."

June looked vexed for a moment. "The message is that I'm tired of Holly making me feel like I'm responsible for all this. It's really bothering me. And it wasn't nice for her to suggest that Paul wasn't happy. It's the happiest time of his life!"

Her voice was very defensive. I stared at her. "You're worried about Paul, aren't you? I saw your face earlier when he was talking about how he wanted to retire from politics. I don't think that was only because you think he's such a great public servant. I think it might have something to do with the fact that you like his position and status in the town. And how that confers on you."

If June sounded defensive before, she was even more so now. "How dare you say such an unpleasant thing! I'm not sure who you think you are, but you have no right to say that."

I was barely listening to her, though. I was suddenly getting a different perspective on June and Paul than I had before. "The thing is, I believe I know exactly why Paul is so upset right now. The reason he hasn't been sleeping and looks so drained all the time. I know why he was avoiding you at your engagement party and why he left as soon as you arrived here earlier today. It's because he thinks you killed Frank and Lindy."

Chapter Twenty-Five

June's eyes widened and her mouth dropped a little. "What?"

"It all makes sense," I said. "We've been looking at everything the wrong way. Yes, Paul stood to lose money if the apartment complex development didn't go through. But he's not the only one who stood to lose out. You did, too."

"You don't know what you're saying." June spoke through gritted teeth.

"Maybe not exactly, but I'm definitely getting the big picture. Maybe you overheard a conversation between Frank and Paul. You realized the significance of the development to Paul and that the project was endangered. You're the one with the big spending habits, or at least that's how it seemed. Paul mentioned always needing more money. But I'm wondering if he needed money to support *your* lifestyle more than his own."

June scoffed. "Paul spends plenty of money on his own."

"Sure. But from what I understand, you're the one who came up with the idea to charter a yacht for a big blowout of a party to celebrate your engagement. It definitely seems like you have the capacity to spend a good deal of money on your own." I glanced at her clothes and purse. While I didn't know much about designers, I could recognize the fact that she wasn't wearing something that came off the rack at the department store.

June seemed both stunned and alarmed, so I continued. "You knew exactly how ethical Frank's always been. After all, you were his wife. You realized there was no way for Paul to persuade Frank to overlook the discovery of human remains on the site. Maybe you also knew there was something a little suspect about Paul's involvement in the site to begin with. You figured the only way to ensure the development went through was if you were to get rid of Frank altogether."

June pushed her way further inside Holly's house, gently shutting the door behind her. Murphy, who'd surprisingly been sleeping, got up and lumbered over near me. I noticed Murphy wasn't his usual, extroverted self. He was very tense, maybe as a reaction to the atmosphere.

June found her voice again. "This is completely ridiculous. You're a librarian, right? I guess that means you read a lot. Clearly, your time spent reading has really sparked your imagination." She gave a coarse laugh.

I said, "Here's what I'm thinking happened. Lindy remembered that you'd called the office to speak with Frank the morning Frank died. Maybe you were planning on stopping by the practice to plead your case that Frank should forget about the remains he'd found on the site. But she told you Frank was out. Maybe you told her to leave him a message . . . that you had to speak with him."

June edged closer to me, as if she wanted to hear every word out of my mouth. Murphy, disliking the proximity, made a grunting noise.

I continued, "Here's where I'm not totally sure what happened. But I *think* Lindy might have been jealous of your relationship with Frank."

June snorted. "What relationship? He was my ex. I'm getting married to someone else."

I shrugged. "Sometimes people aren't totally rational when they love somebody. Lindy mentioned before that she'd been cheated on by a previous man in her life. Whatever the reason, I'm guessing Lindy made a particular note of the fact that you'd called. You murdered Frank at the library. Maybe you realized Frank would never change his mind. It was easier to just shove a stack of bookshelves at him while he was huddled over his research. Perhaps you even noticed what he was working on—that he was further researching the site where he'd found the bones. He wasn't going to give up."

I took a deep breath. Murphy looked at me with concern. "You saw no one was around. You shoved the bookcases down and then took off."

June looked at me with an expressionless look on her face. "Is this what Holly thinks, too?"

"Nope. This is just what I think." I realized June was dangerous. She'd already killed two people and was only going to become more desperate when it came to protecting her secret.

"Well, what you're saying is nonsense."

I said, "You probably saw his car at the library when you drove into the parking lot. And it's not as if Frank was a stranger to the library. It was a natural place for you to look for him. You must have thought your problems were solved when Frank was gone. And that you'd gotten away with it. Sure, the police were asking questions, but it wasn't as if they had honed in on you as the prime suspect. They were probably focused on you because you were Frank's ex-wife. Still, it looked as if you weren't bitter about your divorce at all—after all, you were getting married.

And, in your eyes anyway, marrying the mayor of Charleston was a step up from marrying a relic hunting dentist."

June shook her head. "You don't know what you're talking about."

The deadness of her voice made a shiver go up my spine. Murphy didn't like the tone either. He made a grunt of a growl. Fitz, who hadn't gotten up to greet the visitor, now jumped down off the sofa and padded over next to me, as if backing me up.

I took a deep breath. Grayson and Holly weren't going to be back soon, not with more than one errand. But I'd gone too far to turn back now. "The thing is, Lindy started thinking about your phone call. She thought about the fact that you had a lot to lose, too, if that development didn't work out. Maybe Lindy wondered if, after you'd gotten off the call with her, you'd gone looking for Frank. After all, if he wasn't at the office, he was most likely at the library or at a dig site."

"Listen to you," said June snidely. "Aren't you so smart? Miss Librarian."

"Lindy probably called you. Asked to speak with you."

June rolled her eyes. "Sure. At the break of dawn. She asked me to come by the dental practice."

I raised my eyebrows. "That's very telling that you know that fact. Considering we didn't say anything about it earlier."

June's teeth showed in a snarl and she lunged at me, hands reaching for my neck.

I sidestepped her at the same point that Murphy leaped at June, knocking her off-balance. As June fell to the floor, I sprinted for the door, grabbing at it frantically before finally opening the door and running outside.

Which was when I ran directly into Warner, who apparently had gotten Holly's message, and decided to stop by instead of calling.

Chapter Twenty-Six

I'd barreled right into Warner's chest, and he reflexively put his lanky arms around me. "Ann? What's wrong?"

June came flying out of the house at that moment with a fire extinguisher in her hands and a murderous look in her eyes. When she spotted Warner and me, she realized the game was up. She flung the fire extinguisher to the side and reached in her pocket to pull her car keys out.

Warner snorted. "You're going to have a tough time leaving. Since I'm parked behind you."

June pivoted and sprinted down the street. I pulled out my phone with shaking hands and called the police.

Warner was surprisingly good in an emergency. He ushered me back inside and fixed me a glass of water and a glass of wine. I was shivering still, so he tossed a blanket on me as I huddled on the sofa with Fitz and Murphy. Fitz curled into my lap, looking earnestly at me. Murphy was regarding Warner rather suspiciously, as if he'd suddenly realized not all humans were trustworthy.

Warner perched on a chair nearby and called Holly. His reedy voice was clear as he said, "Holly? Hey. Everything is fine. But I'm at your house and June just tried to kill Ann."

I winced.

"No, she's just fine," he continued cheerfully. "But June is on the loose. We've called the cops, though."

I could already hear the sirens in the background. I took a large sip of wine.

As expected, Holly and Grayson arrived directly after the cops got there. They both gave me a tight hug. Warner was already looking distracted as if he was ready to get out of there.

But there were the police to talk with and give statements to. There was a team of cops out looking for June on foot. There were also police in Holly's driveway, going through June's vehicle. And there were detectives, including Roberts, speaking to all of us.

Warner quickly said, "Sorry, but I've got a dig I need to get to. I was just planning on running by here briefly and then taking off. Can you talk to me first?"

Roberts nodded. "Could you tell me why you were here to begin with?"

Holly interjected, "I called Warner earlier and left him a message saying I wanted to speak with him. I'm really glad I did now." She glanced at him. "I didn't even realize you knew where I lived."

Warner gave her a crooked smile. "I have a good memory. Frank had casually pointed your place out to me when we were driving by one day on the way to a site we were both working."

Roberts made a note in a small notebook. "And why were you so eager to speak with Warner, Holly?"

Holly paused, then gave Warner a rueful look. "I felt like he might be responsible for Frank and Lindy's deaths. His alibi didn't add up. I wanted to find out what he was doing this morning."

"And what *were* you doing?" asked Roberts.

Warner looked uncomfortable. "I was just out grabbing fast food for breakfast and trying to escape my landlord."

"That sounds innocuous enough."

Warner shrugged. "Well, since I was already a suspect, I didn't want to point more attention my way. Which I totally would have done if I'd said I was out driving around when Lindy died." He sighed. "When I listened to Holly's message, I wasn't sure what to think. But I knew I didn't want Holly thinking I'd killed her brother. I had the feeling that's the direction her mind was heading in. I decided it would be better for me to run by her house and talk to her in person. Straighten everything out."

Roberts nodded. "What happened when you arrived?"

"I parked behind one of the cars. I figured it was probably Ann's or Grayson's car. I was on my way to the door when I saw Ann tearing out of the house. Then I saw June following her with a fire extinguisher." He waved his hands around to indicate the general surroundings. "And I didn't see a fire."

"Did it seem to you like June was acting threateningly?"

Warner said, "Oh, yeah. No question. June had murder in her eyes when she came out of the house. Then it was clear she wanted to get out of there. She got her keys out, but stopped when she saw I'd blocked her car in." He gestured toward the window. "I mean, there was no way she could have gotten out without hitting my car and Holly's car. I parked real close behind her." He looked pleased with himself.

Roberts made some more notes. "Okay, thanks. You're free to head on out, if you want to. I might call you later if I need more information."

And with a look of great relief, Warner took off.

Grayson put his arm around me as we sat together on the sofa. Fitz was still on my lap, curled up, but looking at me with a concerned expression on his face.

Roberts gave me a smile. "Are you doing okay?"

I gave him a shaky smile in return. "I'm getting there."

"Could you fill us all in on what happened?" asked Roberts.

"Yes. Grayson and Holly had left in Grayson's car to run errands. So, Holly's car was the only one outside. That's important, because June thought Holly was here alone. She didn't realize Grayson and I were staying with Holly; she thought we were staying in an Airbnb."

"Got it," said Roberts, making more notes.

"I stayed here at the house, reading. When there was a tap at the door, I figured Grayson or Holly had forgotten something, so I got up to get the door. June was standing there."

"Was your first instinct that there was any danger?" asked Roberts.

I shook my head. "I was surprised to see her, of course. But she looked even more surprised to see me."

"Do you think she was planning on hurting Holly?"

Holly shivered a little, and I gave her a reassuring smile.

"I think it was definitely something that was on the table. It seemed to me like June was becoming a little paranoid. That she might have wanted to surprise Holly with a conversation and find out what she actually knew. For all she knew, Paul could have confided his suspicions to Holly. But if she'd been satisfied that Holly didn't know anything, she might have just walked away."

Roberts said, "You think when she saw you standing there at the door, it knocked her a little off-kilter?"

"Sure. Plus, I wondered what she was doing there. It made me think more about what she might be up to. After all, she'd just been at Holly's house minutes before. She hadn't left anything here. So why was she back visiting Holly? Then she told me to leave a snarky message for Holly—something like she didn't appreciate her allegations." I shrugged. "She was definitely agitated."

Roberts said, "You were saying you started thinking more about June's connection to the investigation."

"I think we were mostly focused on the fact that June had been Frank's ex-wife. More of the personal connection. And that was partly right. She knew a lot about Frank—his personality and his ethics and how he approached things." I paused. "I'm guessing you've been investigating the mayor's involvement in the development that Frank was searching."

Roberts just gave me a noncommittal smile.

I continued. "Anyway, she had as much of a financial interest in the development going ahead as Paul did. And she knew Frank wouldn't turn a blind eye to the fact that he'd discovered human remains on the site. He wouldn't have been able to be persuaded to keep his mouth shut—not for anything."

"The only way to keep him quiet was to shut him up permanently," said Holly quietly.

"Right. We know June is a big spender. She was motivated to make sure that development moved forward." I suddenly felt very sad. Frank had wanted to do the right thing. June had been determined to do the wrong thing. He never had a chance. I glanced over at Holly and she gave me a small smile.

A police officer came in from outside. He said to Roberts, "We've discovered what appears to be the murder weapon from the dental office."

Roberts nodded. "In the suspect's car?"

The officer bobbed his head and went back outside.

Holly's smile broadened now. "Real evidence."

Roberts said, "Right. Especially helpful, since what we're dealing with now is conjecture."

I said, "Did you get good images from the library exterior cameras? You'd mentioned the cameras the last time we saw you."

Roberts shook his head. "The cameras, unfortunately, weren't very helpful. It's good that we have what seems to be the murder weapon. Okay, so we covered June and Frank. What was your take on why June murdered Lindy Baker?"

I said, "June called over to the office the morning Frank died, trying to speak with him. Maybe Lindy started thinking more about that later. She could have contacted June to question her about it. Once June thought of Lindy as a threat, it was all over."

Holly said in a deceptively languid tone, "I can't imagine what June thought I knew."

I shrugged. "June was becoming increasingly desperate to protect herself. She had a lot to lose. I think her paranoia was working against her. She thought you were pushing her too much—that you knew something. She came over to see what you actually knew. She saw a car was gone and figured Grayson and I were gone and she could approach Holly privately."

Roberts said, "What do you think June thought Holly was pushing too hard on?"

"June was pretty upset when Holly asked her if Paul was all right," noted Grayson.

I nodded. "She got really defensive about him. I think the reason Paul looked so ill is because he suspected his fiancée was potentially his best friend's murderer."

Roberts got a phone call and stepped out the door for a moment to take it. I took another sip of my glass of wine, feeling myself start to relax a little here with my friends and with the safety of the police around us.

When Roberts came back in, he was smiling a smile of grim satisfaction. "They picked her up. You won't have to worry about June anymore."

Holly's shoulders slumped with relief. I felt myself relaxing even more.

"It's over," said Holly.

Chapter Twenty-Seven

It was actually over in more ways than one. Grayson and I decided to head back to Whitby the next morning. That last night in Charleston, though, we had a celebration of sorts . . . Holly had insisted on it. She said that even though she was still distraught over her brother's death, she was glad that justice had been done—and that I had survived my unexpected encounter with June. Grayson had grimly agreed that he wanted to drink to that. And so we had. Holly played music from a great playlist, we celebrated June's arrest, and the animals looked on with tolerant bewilderment. Holly called her parents and gave them the good news.

Holly gave us a big hug as we left the next day. "Thank you," she said. "I don't know what I'd have done if you hadn't been here."

We thanked her for our stay and headed off with Fitz from the coast back to the mountains. We were quiet most of the way home, thinking about everything that had taken place.

Grayson said, "I'm so glad you're okay, Ann. I can't believe how close I came to losing you back there."

I smiled at him. "All's well that ends well. Although I think I might write Warner a little thank-you note. He helped out by showing up when he did—and by blocking June's car."

Grayson dropped by my house and helped me carry my suitcase, Fitz, and a couple of small bags into the house. He gave me a tight hug. "See you tomorrow?" He asked before heading back to his place. I nodded.

Fitz seemed very chipper about being back in his usual stomping grounds. He immediately padded to his favorite sunbeam, gave me a feline smile, bathed himself, and fell asleep.

I unpacked and got a load of laundry started before calling Wilson at the library. I had the feeling my manager was going to be delighted that I was home a bit early.

"Ann? Everything all right? Are you back home?" he asked sharply.

I wasn't quite sure which question to answer first. But they made me smile. It was good to be needed, good to be missed. Wilson's tone made it sound as if he was concerned that I maybe had decided to stay in Charleston.

"I'm back home," I said. "We wrapped things up a little early. I was just wondering if you wanted to add me to the schedule for tomorrow. Or, if you're fully staffed, I can just do some errands and things here."

Wilson's relief was palpable as it came through the phone. "Oh, I'm so glad you're back. I have a lot of respect for our staff and do find them quite capable. But they don't seem to do things exactly the way you do, Ann. It'll be good to have you work tomorrow, fully staffed or not."

"I'll be there, then."

"Good." Wilson's voice was distracted, and I could tell he was looking at the next thing on his list. Then he briefly seemed to realize niceties should probably be observed. "And how was your trip? Did you and Grayson have a pleasant time in Charleston?"

"It's a beautiful city. I loved seeing the sights there. Perhaps it wasn't quite as restful as I thought it might be."

"You need a vacation from your vacation?" asked Wilson with a chuckle. "Sounds like the perfect reason to get back to work.

And it was. The next morning when I walked into the library, I saw Zelda fussing at a patron for asking too many questions, Luna directing a wildly original toddler storytime, and a couple of copiers that weren't working. A grin spread across my face at being home.

About the Author

Elizabeth writes the Southern Quilting mysteries and Memphis Barbeque mysteries for Penguin Random House and the Myrtle Clover series for Midnight Ink and independently. She blogs at ElizabethSpannCraig.com/blog, named by Writer's Digest as one of the 101 Best Websites for Writers. Elizabeth makes her home in Matthews, North Carolina, with her husband. She's the mother of two.

Sign up for Elizabeth's free newsletter to stay updated on releases:

https://bit.ly/2xZUXqO

This and That

I love hearing from my readers. You can find me on Facebook as Elizabeth Spann Craig Author, on Twitter as elizabethscraig, on my website at elizabethspanncraig.com, and by email at elizabethspanncraig@gmail.com.

Thanks so much for reading my book...I appreciate it. If you enjoyed the story, would you please leave a short review on the site where you purchased it? Just a few words would be great. Not only do I feel encouraged reading them, but they also help other readers discover my books. Thank you!

Did you know my books are available in print and ebook formats? Most of the Myrtle Clover series is available in audio and some of the Southern Quilting mysteries are. Find the audiobooks here: https://elizabethspanncraig.com/audio/

Please follow me on BookBub for my reading recommendations and release notifications.

I'd also like to thank some folks who helped me put this book together. Thanks to my cover designer, Karri Klawiter, for her awesome covers. Thanks to my editor, Judy Beatty for her help. Thanks to beta readers Amanda Arrieta, Rebecca Wahr, Cassie Kelley, and Dan Harris for all of their helpful suggestions and careful reading. Thanks to my ARC readers for helping to spread the word. Thanks, as always, to my family and readers.

Other Works by Elizabeth

Myrtle Clover Series in Order (be sure to look for the Myrtle series in audio, ebook, and print):

Pretty is as Pretty Dies
Progressive Dinner Deadly
A Dyeing Shame
A Body in the Backyard
Death at a Drop-In
A Body at Book Club
Death Pays a Visit
A Body at Bunco
Murder on Opening Night
Cruising for Murder
Cooking is Murder
A Body in the Trunk
Cleaning is Murder
Edit to Death
Hushed Up
A Body in the Attic
Murder on the Ballot
Death of a Suitor
A Dash of Murder
Death at a Diner
A Myrtle Clover Christmas
Murder at a Yard Sale (2023)

Southern Quilting Mysteries in Order:

Quilt or Innocence

Knot What it Seams

Quilt Trip

Shear Trouble

Tying the Knot

Patch of Trouble

Fall to Pieces

Rest in Pieces

On Pins and Needles

Fit to be Tied

Embroidering the Truth

Knot a Clue

Quilt-Ridden

Needled to Death

A Notion to Murder

Crosspatch

Behind the Seams

Quilt Complex (2023)

The Village Library Mysteries in Order (Debuting 2019):

Checked Out

Overdue

Borrowed Time

Hush-Hush

Where There's a Will

Frictional Characters

Spine Tingling

A Novel Idea

End of Story

Memphis Barbeque Mysteries in Order (Written as Riley Adams):
Delicious and Suspicious
Finger Lickin' Dead
Hickory Smoked Homicide
Rubbed Out
And a standalone "cozy zombie" novel: Race to Refuge, written as Liz Craig

Printed in Great Britain
by Amazon